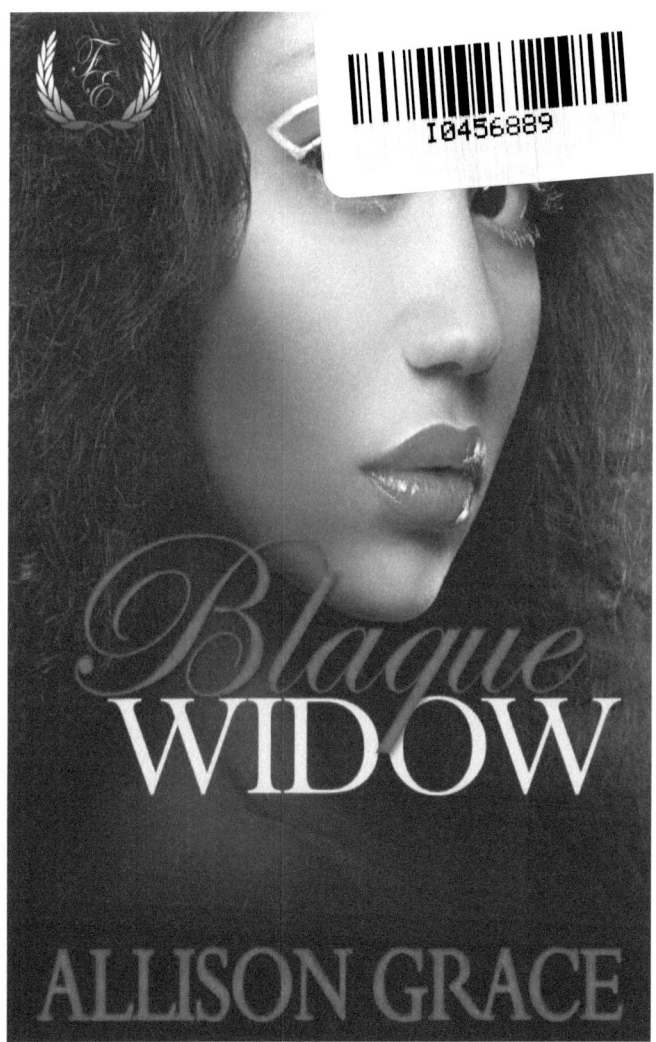

I0456889

Blaque Widow

Allison Grace

Blaque Widow   **Allison Grace**

Cover Concept and Design by

Brittani Williams

Trend Setters Publications Creative

Editing by Joy Hammond Nelson

ISBN-13: 978-0-9830481-8-3

ISBN-10: 0-9830481-8-5

www.fullofessence.com

For all orders and inquiries, please contact

fullofessence@gmail.com

Enjoy other novels by Allison Grace

Broken Promises Never Mend

Bound by Lies

Bittersweet

Christmas Kisses (a holiday short story)

All She Wants for Christmas is Love (a holiday
short story)

Prepaid Mistress 1 & 2

Bitch Clique Reloaded

Blaque Widow

Allison Grace

<u>Acknowledgements</u>

GOD

My parents Norman & Grace – Your support in this means the world to me. I am who I am because of you.

My Children Jay & Mikey- You give me purpose. Thank you for loving me unconditionally.

Steve, Monique & Jon—the best siblings ever. Love always!

To my friends, THANK YOU!

To my fans/supporters, I appreciate all the love you have given me and I hope that you will continue to follow my journey. It's only the beginning of a journey that I plan to continue!

My love, thank you for being my #1 fan. You inspired me to be greater than the day before.

Whoever I "forgot," please know I love you still-Charge It to My Head and Not My Heart!

Much Love Always

Allison Grace

Blaque Widow   **Allison Grace**

A Note from the Author

Here we are again.

If you are reading this, then you've taken the time to read one of my works. I thank you so much and I know you all have been waiting for a few things from me. I decided to bring this out of the attic and dust it off. This story is darker than most stories I've written and deals with something many won't address, especially women of color deal. It takes us to a very different place emotionally. I hope it reaches you and inspires you as it did me.

Once again, I thank you for continuing to read my works and I hope I can thrill you yet again. Your support is indelible and I love you all!

Blaque Widow   Allison Grace

Dedication

Brandon...

Everything happened for a reason,

including US

Blaque Widow

Allison Grace

Prologue

 I took the unsuspecting man by the hand and led him downstairs towards the basement. My manicured hands clasped his until I felt the flesh beneath my fingertips tingle. I was frightened but excited and my heart beat loud enough to resemble African drums.

It was dark but I wanted our experience to be memorable. I cared less about his pleasure and more about mine. I was the only one that mattered. My victim, although I knew of him, wasn't someone that I knew personally. He was someone that came back and forth every once in a while and was familiar to me only by face.

It only made sense that he was the one that I fucked randomly. I had no immediate connection to him. This made it easier to carry out the task. All I cared about was his sex. The truth of the matter was that I traded one addiction for another and he was just what I needed to fill my void.

As we entered my usual spot, his large fingers gripped me from behind and I felt his warm breath against my neck as he shadowed my footsteps. Our steps were in sync as we each took a step downstairs into his impending doom. We walked until we set our eyes upon a piece of furniture to rest upon. It was my favorite couch.

It was a rusty brown couch that rested up against a wall. Several red spots decorated it to show it had been used recently. I paid no attention to that evidence and I hoped he didn't either. I just wanted him to get comfortable so I could shake him out of his zone.

Using a cell phone as a lamp to guide us, I found an overhead light switch. It was dim but it was all we could use to see each other. Slight silhouettes of our bodies were all that was seen in the faint light of the lamp. My curves stood out the most. My black skirt rose high above my thigh and the black lace garter I wore was revealed to be twisted. I didn't care for I declined to adjust it.

"Are you okay with us being down here?" I said to my latest victim Lance Myers. I walked over to him from where the wall was and stood there watching him. My eyes adjusted to the darkness while his struggled horribly. He tried to look around but the crepuscule wouldn't allow him.

All of what he saw was mostly shadows. We found the couch and I stood over him causing my curves to take over his vision. My bra was white lace and my mocha nipples stood erect cushioned by areolas of the same shade. His eyes watched as I massaged them to make them harder beneath the sheer material. They stood at attention as my fingers tweaked and pulled them to erection.

"Yeah, yeah I'm good Taryn. I just want you to do what you promised me. I have to be home but you looked too good to resist. I always loved a thick woman. My wife is..."

As he aimlessly talked about his spouse, I felt a rage engulf my body. My hand raised above my head and came down upon him. I slapped him in the face and scratched him in the process. He didn't care. He loved the abuse. It caused his erection to grow harder than a roll of quarters.

"Shut the fuck up about your wife. You want me to suck and fuck you? The stipulation is I'm your bitch. No mention of any other pussy but mine. Is that clear?"

I pushed him down on the couch and the springs responded to the pressure. As he adjusted himself under my weight, nothing was heard but squeaking and his heavy breathing.

I realized that I had him shook and scared that he wouldn't be able to get the sex that I promised him. He had been waiting for months to try to fuck me but I kept giving him my ass to kiss. It was all a part of the plan. Make him want me so much that he would be willing to do anything and forego all sense of self. It had finally happened.

All he could do was nod his head. Feeling his erection deep within my pussy aroused me due to the radiating heat. Drips of pussy juice escaped and landed on his crotch. I wore no panties and felt they were a waste of time and money. They ended up coming off eventually so why bother.

Leaning back, I pulled at his waistline removing his belt buckle. He pushed my hand away and opened his jeans button. I felt my way around his waist and he eased up so he could pull his pants down around his ankles. As soon as he did, his dick bounced out of his boxers like a staff on a flagpole.

"Damn, ready for me already are you? Good. I don't like to wait for anything." I adjusted myself and placed his chocolate dick deep within the folds of my pussy.

It was like stirring macaroni and cheese. The sounds of him deep within my walls felt like heaven. Thick remnants of my juices oozed down the shaft of his erection. It felt so good that I threw my head back and began riding him hard like a mechanical bull.

"Ohhh shit. Damn...Oh my God you feel good." Lance leaned his head back on the back of the couch and allowed me to take control. His thick hands gripped my waist causing indents in the side of my hips. I twerked my ample ass on his shaft and caused a tingling sensation within my stomach.

I literally felt every inch of him inside of me. The churning of our juices blending was heard softly and moisture was seen oozing from the bottom of my pussy.

I bounced on him hard and he grunted as his hard dick entered my cavity. My love tunnel responded to every thrust and the color changed from clear to thick as he hit my spot causing me to cum.

"Uh uh yeah, oh shit damn you gon' make me cum." Lance gripped my dress tightly and pulled out my left breast. His tongue traced the outside of my mocha areola, which had tiny bumps surrounding it. That happened when I got aroused.

I felt my body move like waves onto his and give way to the next orgasm that approached. I dove forward and applied more pressure onto his dick. Using my hand as leverage on the back of the couch, I rode him hard. The feeling that I gave him reflected on his face and he grimaced as if struggling to hold back. He was in bliss. So much so that he didn't notice me sticking my hand in a piece of torn fabric of the worn down couch and pulling out a knuckle knife that was hidden. It cushioned my hands and Lance continued to be oblivious of the activities being plotted against him.

The crook of my left arm cradled his neck ever so slightly and I brought my lips to his. It was as if we were exchanging breaths when in fact I began the process of taking his soul. He continued to thrust upward into my canal and he hit my g spot just as his tongue invaded my mouth. Upon climax, I felt hot spurts shoot within me as he reached his peak.

At that moment, I brought my right hand up and stabbed him in the back of his neck so deep that his scream was stuck in his throat. Blood escaped and I tasted the blood on my tongue arousing me further. He thrust his waist up fiercely trying to escape the hold of death that gripped him.

Even though I already achieved an orgasm, the fact that it felt like he was still fucking me literally to the death turned me on. I maintained the hold on him until he grew limp in my hands.

"Shhhhhhhh I told you I would be more than you could handle," I whispered softly in his ear as his breath faded like a clock running out of batteries. The knife had pierced his carotid artery and punctured his windpipe. He had no control over what was going on with him.

His eyes stared blankly into mine and appeared hollow. Even in the dark, I could see his blank stare. I knew he was gone. Crimson fluid seeped through his nostrils and out of the side of his mouth. I removed the knife slowly and wiped it on the back of the couch with remnants of his DNA joining others whose fate was left and lost in my hands.

I placed the knife in the hidden slit behind the couch and sighed. My work was done. Both of us achieved orgasm and I removed myself from on top of him.

Gobs of semen dripped down my leg and I walked over to the corner of the basement where there was a bathroom. I needed to clean up and not leave any of his DNA inside of me. I reached up and pulled a string located in the middle of the room and the light came on. Roaches and spiders scurried everywhere upon being revealed.

I had to relieve myself. I wanted to take a shower but that would have to do for the moment. I found myself on the toilet and urinated. The remainder of semen leaked out and I spotted a hot water bottle that sat on the side of the sink. I turned on the faucet and let the water run until it was scalding. I placed some water inside of it and reached under the sink to retrieve a bottle of vinegar.

Pouring some into the hot water, I shook it up so it all came together as a cleansing solution. I began to douche my pussy so as to remove the remainder of his babies. Having babies wasn't an option right then, if at all, but I more so wanted any signs of him out of me. There was to be no evidence of the encounter. Just as I was finishing up, my cell phone rang.

"Is the deed done?" the voice said on the other end of the line. It was authoritative and to the point. There wasn't so much as a hello.

"Yes I am just getting cleaned up. I'm leaving so you can clean up," I said drying myself with a dark blue terry cloth towel that was hung in the bathroom.

"I will be there in fifteen minutes."

Click. The phone call ended.

Three Years Earlier

<u>For Better or Worse</u>

And by the powers vested in me I now pronounce you husband and wife. I am pleased to announce for the first time anywhere, Mr. and Mrs. Devon Hardy," the reverend said as he smiled at my husband and me.

"You may now kiss your bride," he continued. Devon removed the veil from my face and my ruby red lipstick shimmered in the sunlight. It was time to seal our union with a kiss. The lips of my new husband touched mine and his wet tongue slithered into my mouth and began to dance with my own tongue.

"Okay. Save some for the honeymoon," was shouted from the audience.

I was truly happy. My eyes fluttered as I thought of the life that we would have together. At the reception however, I got the hint on what my life would entail. I danced with my father during the father/daughter dance and my cousin who also raised me cut in briefly. His hand caressed my waist and he whispered to me how proud of me he was. A few minutes into the dance, I was almost hoisted up into the air as my new husband grabbed me harshly from him. He wanted his time with me. In doing so, he ripped my wedding dress as he stepped on it when he dragged me.

"Ouch baby. What's wrong? That was Javon my cousin from my dad's side." I caressed his face and he smiled forcibly while removing my hand by my wrist causing pain to me. I glanced around to see who was watching the violent exchange. Since it was our wedding that would be everyone as I was being photographed and there was video.

"I don't give a fuck who it is. No one touches you like that in my presence. You are mine. Then. Now. Always," he whispered in my ear and bit my lobe not caring that he was hurting me. To save face, I cried with a smile on my face. Everyone commented to me how I looked so happy but they had no idea of the pain I endured. No one knew how much pain I would endure later on.

There were beatings, bruises, and battles. There was that time when he locked his key in the car a week after we married and he backhanded me causing me to lose a tooth. I had to tell the dentist that when I was at my wedding the microphone hit my tooth loosening it and I had an apple that caused it to fall out. I thought things would change but within months, that would prove to be as much of a lie as what my marriage was turning out to be.

I had met my husband at a lounge four years earlier when I signed up for speed dating. It was something I never thought I would be able to do but it worked for us. Now there we were married. The best was yet to come. That was until it left.

As fast as it came, things changed and I was brought back to reality. As much as I prayed for things to change for the better, they changed for the worse. I didn't know that this was what "for better or worse" felt like.

"I'm on my way home from work. What the fuck you been doing all day?"

My husband Devon called me several times a day and harassed me. The opportunity always presented itself for him to call our home. I hated talking to him but believed in submitting to my husband so I answered each and every phone call with a hint of glee in my voice.

"I, I am just about to finish up dinner. It will be ready by the time you get home," I said as I added some more salt and pepper to the beef stew I had simmering on the stove. The aroma of dinner wafted into the hallway and I heard a few neighbors commenting on the scent that traveled easily into the hallway of our one bedroom apartment building.

We lived on the first floor and everything traveled outside of our door. Aromas, sounds, everything. Especially sounds of us arguing. The previous night was the worst it had been in a long time. We usually fought and argued several times a week. I guess I had been doing things right until then.

"Good. When I come home, I want the remote, beer, dinner, and head. In that order." Devon always said what he meant. I learned to adapt to his behavior as best as possible. I accepted what was and wanted to be the best woman possible for him. I did what I could to keep my man.

The phone hung up and I placed it back on the base. I continued to stir the pot and looked at the microwave clock behind me. I wanted to get ready before he arrived home. I had some news to tell him.

Placing the pot on low, I ran into the bedroom and grabbed a towel. I stripped, leaving my house dress on the floor, and ran into the bathroom. My breasts jiggled as I made my way. I wanted to freshen up before my husband came home. Turning on the water, I hopped right in regardless of the temperature. My fair skin reddened when I realized I hadn't regulated it and it was scalding hot. I didn't care.

Lately he had been complaining about my body odor and I needed to make sure I was extra clean for him. All the weight I gained had prompted a slight smell. I noticed it myself especially around ovulation. My pheromones even turned myself on at times.

I placed some soap on a loofah and began scrubbing my skin fiercely until there were splotches of red appearing. I needed things to be like they used to be when we got married. Things had changed so much and fast.

I rinsed myself off and stepped out of the tub. My feet nestled comfortably against the plush orange carpet beneath my feet. I tossed the damp towel on the sink and put on my black lace panties one foot at a time. I almost lost my balance when my left foot hit the waist of my panties as I was putting them on. The bathroom clock dinged and I knew it was six o clock. My husband was on his way home. I quickly put my bra on and threw on my leggings and a long tee shirt.

I ran out of the bathroom but not before I sprayed some perfume on my body and ran my hands through my hair. It was already short and curly so I had nothing special to do to it. I ran to the kitchen just in time to smell the food on the stove catching. I turned it off and stirred it just as Devon walked in through the door.

"I'm home," he said stoically.

I wiped my hand on a dishrag and ran to the door to greet my husband. He dropped his book bag on the floor and stepped out of his shoes. I stood up on my tiptoes to reach up and kiss him but my mouth met air as I watched him walk right past me. I picked up his book bag and placed it on the doorknob.

"Hi, Devon. Did you have a good day at work baby?"

My husband looked at me with a blank stare as if he was waiting on something. I totally forgot briefly, what he asked for when he spoke before leaving work. I ran to the refrigerator and got a Heineken beer for him opening it. The top fell to the floor and tinkered as it landed right side up. I left it there hoping to remember it later before one or both of us stepped on it.

"I'm sorry baby. Here you go." I handed him the beer and he took it in his hand while I reached over and retrieved the remote. I gave it to him and he smirked at me.

"When is dinner going to be ready?"

"It already is. When you are finished with your first beer, I can have it for you on a tray. Just let me know when." I forced a smile trying not to ignite the anger that often rose up inside of him without warning.

It was because of him that I ended up cutting my hair. During a physical altercation over a text message he viewed on my phone, Devon dragged me through the house by my hair. Devon didn't care.

My lovely ebony hair scattered all around the living room and hallway. Clumps of it wrapped itself around his fist while I sat with my knees towards my chest praying he would stop hurting me. The text message was simply a notification from Instagram saying that one of my followers called me his "Woman Crush Wednesday."

Once Devon got wind of it, he wanted to know who the person was and if we had been having sex. I denied it and he tossed me out on my ass by my hair. Because of the breakage, I had to cut my hair in a short sleek style.

I ran my hands over my scalp and allowed my natural curls to embrace my fingers. It felt good to feel growth even if it was in my hair. I was still in a fragile emotional state.

"I'm ready for dinner Taryn. The game is coming on so don't take forever!" Devon bellowed from the living room.

I heard the recliner extend and I knew he had his feet up awaiting his meal. I pulled a plate from the dishwasher and spooned some rice into the center. I then placed some of the beef stew onto the plate right on top of the rice making sure the edges weren't littered with gravy.

Carrots, peas, and potatoes decorated the plate and I wrapped up a fork with a napkin and grabbed another beer for my husband. I wanted to do everything right this time. I walked out smiling and handed him the tray while still holding his beer. I opened it and placed it next to him taking up the old bottle that he already drank.

"I hope dinner is to your liking. I remember you saying you wanted beef stew the other day."

I stepped to the side as I watched him take the fork and dip into the plate. He placed

it into his mouth and yelped like an injured dog.
It was too hot and I heard him grumble under
his breath. I lost mine.

"It's fine. I want to watch the game in
peace."

I retreated silently as I watched him stuff
more food into his mouth. I once loved him so
much but it was my fault for thinking I could
change a man that already had issues. If only I
knew just how deep seeded, they were.

#####

Hours later, it was time to give him the
rest of what he requested. I showered again
right after he did and found him in bed. I

cuddled up with my back to him and drops of water trickled down my spine. The coolness was soon replaced by Devon's warm breath on my neck. He wanted sex. I wanted him to go away. I was scared of him and I had every reason to be. Every time he touched me, it caused me to cry. Love wasn't supposed to hurt but I didn't want to give up before I even gave it a chance.

"You handled that to my liking?" Devon grunted at me while poking me harshly in my back with his dick. It didn't take much to arouse him. A full belly and some beer usually did the trick. After getting married, I finally learned something right when it came to him.

"Yes it's ready for you Devon," I said as I rolled over onto my back.

He climbed on top of me and roughly kissed my lips. His moustache scratched the top of my lip and I felt tiny bumps forming under my nose. I moved my face to my left side and stared at the window. I wondered what was going on outside of those four walls.

I felt him roughly stick his fingers inside of me and pull them out. He placed his fingers under his own nose, sniffed, and then wiped his fingertips on my lips but not before stuffing them in my mouth. I tasted sweet yet tart.

"That's how a bitch is supposed to smell and taste. Don't no nigga want to fuck a stink pussy."

I felt his manhood grow harder beneath me. That was all the foreplay I was allowed as I felt him press deeper into my pubic bone until he found the entrance to my canal. I wasn't wet but I wasn't dry either.

As I watched the lights above me flicker, I counted seven hundred and thirty nine tiles on the ceiling. That was the amount of tiles that were above me. If they could talk, they would have yelled out to me not to marry this man. I loved him. Or so I made myself believe. I thought all this while he pounded his dick inside of me. To say I wasn't impressed was an understatement.

"Uhh Taryn, this some good pussy. Move your fat ass," my husband directed me to move so he could cum. I simply opened my legs wider and moaned slightly making him feel as if he had some effect on me. I felt him thrusting inside of me roughly and I gripped his back. Beads of sweat dropped from his forehead onto my neck and face. I closed my eyes and pretended that I wasn't even there.

"Ooh yeah. Right there. Give it to me Devon," I said in faux excitement.

My monotonous tone was apparent but he overlooked it as his thighs dug deeper into mine. His jackhammer method of sexing me indicated that he was only concerned with his own pleasure. That little bit of encouragement was all he needed to hear. I felt his erection grow inside of me and his movement sped up. Hot spurts were ejected inside of me and he grunted with each thrust. Devon collapsed on top of me as sweat fell from his forehead onto my breasts.

"Did you like that baby? It felt good?" I asked breathing slowly.

His weight was crushing my voluptuous frame and I wanted him off me. I couldn't stand him touching me for too long.

"That shit was good. Better than the last time," he said as he wiped his face and remained on my breast. I tried to get up but he held my waist.

"Where the fuck you think you're going? You're gonna sit and simmer in my scent."

He pressed down on my bladder with his head making it known that he wasn't moving. I continued to count the ceiling tiles. I had to get rid of the pain that I was enduring. He was torturing me. This wasn't the man I married but the signs were there immediately after we said I do. I was just too naïve to pay attention to them.

A Kiss Before Dying

The next day Devon left early for work and I ushered him out of the door. As soon as I did, I stuffed my face with the last bit of marshmallows I had hidden in the pantry and washed it down with the Coca-Cola that I had sitting by my side.

Ever since we got married, my size 10 frame had quickly added on more numbers. I chalked it up to being happy but the truth of the matter was I was very unhappy. I found comfort in food and it got comfortable on me.

My fingers were sticky and I wiped them on my blue and white polka dot pajamas. The remote rested comfortably on my breasts, which were covered simply by a V-neck tee shirt. My favorite soap opera was on and I couldn't miss a thing. The phone rang and I looked at it with disgust.

"Hello," I said in a soft voice hoping the person on the other end would believe I was asleep.

"Taryn, it's Mommy. Didn't I ask you if you could come over and help me take these clothes to the Salvation Army? I'm going to end up tossing them away if you don't want them," my mother Edith said as I surveyed my living room.

I kept the place spotless when Devon was around but right before he came home, I went on a cleaning spree. I needed to stop doing that before one day he came home unannounced. I placed a few chips in my mouth and wiped my cheesy hands on my pajama pants.

"Momma I said to ask Kenton to do it. He's the one that promised you anyway. I never agreed on it and since y'all two are such good friends utilize him."

"Devon is your husband and it's your job to take care of his every need. You don't want him straying like your daddy. That muthafucka was a rolling boulder." Edith inhaled the cigarette that she was smoking and I heard her blow out the smoke into the phone.

"He is just like any other man that I dated. The only thing is I married this one against my better judgment. I need to quit listening to you. You've done nothing but fuck up my plans Mother. I should have stayed with Kenton but you wanted him to yourself."

I grew annoyed that my mother pretty much forced me into the hands of a man that didn't have anything going for him other than a decent sized dick. He lied about everything else and my mother believed it.

"Do you miss Kenton?" she asked me as thoughts of him entered my mind. I hated how she still kept in contact with my ex fiancé. It was her fault that our relationship ended.

"No, I miss him like a hooker misses an STD...I'm happy he's gone and out of my life. He preferred you anyway. No need for me to have held on to what wasn't mine. Right Mother?"

"I thought you both would want to come together and see me for old times' sake. Maybe it could inspire you to lose some weight and he would take you back."

Edith's words stung like microscopic bullets. My body jerked back and I pulled the phone from my ear as if it radiated the heat from an oven. It was those words that caused me to feel the way I did about her and Kenton.

It was bad enough the man I married found fault with me and how I looked but the woman that birthed me did also. It was moments like this that I wished that God would come and take her life. Some women don't deserve to be parents. They don't deserve to carry life and bring it forth because they drain the life that they do provide out of what's left of the living.

"Edith," I said through clenched teeth, "I don't want to be with Kenton, nor do I want to have anything to do with him but the next time you see him, fuck him and tell me later how it was!"

I promptly hung up the phone and walked into the kitchen. Anger welled up inside of me and I stared blindly at the cabinets to see what the next thing would be to enter my mouth. The clock shone on the microwave and I knew I needed to clean up and be the wife that I hated to be.

The phone rang incessantly without breaks and I knew that was my mother calling back to yell at me for the disrespect. She refused to back down. I didn't mean it. It was my breaking point. Ever since I got married, my weight was something that I had dealt with. It was a problem that I endured all my life.

From the age of thirteen, I had endured torture from family, friends, and acquaintances. It was because of my weight that I decided to work from home. It was only part time but it was helping taking the edge off the bills. I was tired of Devon buying something as small as my sanitary napkins. If I ran out and didn't have enough money left from the small allowance he provided me then I resorted to wrapping toilet paper. Things got messy and I had to make some changes.

After bleaching my clothes because of one too many accidents, he agreed. Someone advertised in the newspaper for a customer service representative at a cable company. The benefit would be the ability to work from home and minimize the interaction with the public. The pay rate would be the same as if I was in the office but I would have nothing more to do but to handle business accordingly.

I told Devon about it and he agreed so long as it didn't interfere with what he called "quality time" that he demanded when he got home. I couldn't be happier that I was making some money and getting some peace in the process.

Three days a week at 8:45 a.m., after Devon left for work, I logged into the switchboard from my laptop and placed the headphones on my head. With a cup of coffee and a box of donuts, I began my day fielding calls and answering questions about cable channels. Since I spent the majority of my time watching television I was very well versed on what the customers wanted and needed.

I was twenty-nine years old, no kids, and married to who I assumed was the love of my life. I was set to have my birthday in less than a year. My skin was the color of an almond but it was dry due to bouts of eczema. I hated water and drank all things with caffeine even though I knew the repercussions of such an addiction.

I had an addictive personality and that's what made it okay for me to have kept Devon. He showed me the most attention and was what I felt love was. My favorite drink was Coke. A perfect name for an addictive habit that caused me to consume more than a dozen cans a day until I met Devon.

Before we married, my closet held nothing but pajamas and my shoes had no variety in them. There weren't any stilettos or even sneakers for all my money was spent on food. It became my addiction. I lived to eat. My home became my refuge and food became my haven. Mounds of junk food spilled out onto the cabinets beneath. I usually ate what I found. Day old food lingered in packages half eaten.

When it was close to payday and I had no food leftover I resorted to that which I found.

When I first met Devon that had to change. I tossed everything away. He couldn't see the state that I was living in. I decided that I wanted to at least appear normal to him. I drank more water and quit eating so much junk food even though when I was experiencing premenstrual cramps I had to have chocolate by the loads. It was my refuge.

He loved me, he said, despite my weight. He loved my curves and when he made love to me, I felt like Naomi Campbell. No matter what he saw, I still felt like Precious. I looked in the mirror and I saw someone that was ugly, fat, and unattractive so I clung more to him for the validation that he gave me.

After I married, my addiction became Devon. I lived and breathed him. He was the reason why I woke up every day and my goal was to please him. He was my all and could do no wrong in my eyes.

I hated cleaning but Devon was a neat freak so I had to learn to like it. I was meticulous with it. I even found things to clean that weren't dirty. He even said I was dirty at times. His favorite part to insult was my pussy.

The first time he told me that I carried an odor I denied it. We didn't have sex. I felt some sort of way. After the second time I was convinced and got some bleach and mixed it with soap. I took my toothbrush and wrapped a washcloth around it. I dipped it in my homemade cleansing solution and inserted it inside of me.

Little did I know that I was throwing off my own Ph-balance and destroying the lining of my vagina. When I got an infection a few weeks later, Devon swore to me that I was cheating. He demanded that he be in the examining room when my gynecologist broke the news to me.

Once he found out about the infection, he swore I was cheating on him and he watched every move. He didn't let up until it quickly dissolved with medication and clearance from his own physician.

I hated how I depended on him but the job gave me the security and confidence I needed. The reason being that I didn't have to interact with anyone and I could be who I wanted to be. I loved that I didn't have to be around people but then I dreaded what my life had become. I only worked part time because my attention had to be on my husband. He demanded it.

So I got myself ready for work. After sending Devon off to work of course, I busied myself and turned on the coffee pot ready to begin my shift. My mother always called early in the morning as if I was a child and not able to get out of bed. I hadn't reached that point of obesity yet. It was close.

Tipping the scales at almost three hundred pounds I knew I wanted to lose weight but wasn't sure how to go about it. Devon said he liked the way I looked but still didn't pay any attention to me. It was as if he didn't want me but didn't want anyone else to either.

At least we had sex, which was more than I could say for some of my other married friends. At least twice a week I bent my fat ass over and allowed Devon to pound into me until he nut all over my back. He never held me close and rarely kissed me. No real intimacy but I was still able to climax. I asked to get on top so I could kiss him and feel him more but he denied that request. His reasoning was so that he could see my ass shake. That made me smile because at least he saw something in me that turned him on.

In that, I felt confident that our relationship was still okay. I read in so many self-help books that once they don't want to have sex with you, then it's over. My weight was my problem. I got comfortable after we married. When I got comfortable, he got uncomfortable. The more ridicule I received, the more I ate and the more I ate the fatter I got. The fatter I got, the less interested I was in life.

It was a horrible cycle that continued over and over on a daily basis. I decided that when I was truly tired of people fucking with me, I would make a change. As much as I loved my husband, I knew he wasn't my happily ever after. He proved it time and time again with his treatment of me. I didn't know if I believed in those anymore. If my happily ever after truly existed, it would have to come in the form of something or someone else.

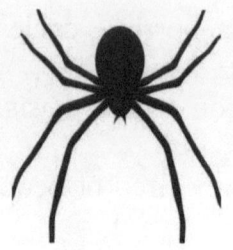

<u>Bottoms Up</u>

ello, thank you for calling CompuVision. This is Taryn how may I help you today," I said as I answered the phone. My headset rested comfortably on my head and I took a sip of coffee. It was 9:07am and this was my first call. I had to close my internet browser, which was open to the latest gossip on Media Takeout.

"Yeah just tell me how much my bill is before I get cut off," he caller spoke abruptly.

There was no greeting. Even though I detected rudeness, there was something about his voice that turned me on.

"Uh sir I need to know your first and last name in order to access the account. Also please provide the number that's associated with the account," I said as I laid on the professionalism thick. I knew a lot of my calls were monitored for quality assurance, especially since I worked from home.

"Asher, Asher Rollins. My address is 348 East 116th Street in New York and my phone number is 212-543-9542."

I minimized my tabloid website and pulled up the appropriate screen in order to assist the customer on the phone. As obnoxious as he sounded, he made something inside of me want to know who he was. I plugged his number into the online database and read the notes in his account. It was supposed to be disconnected by noon that day but he submitted payment.

"Thank you Mr. Rollins. I see from your account that you are scheduled for a disconnection but it's been halted while it clears. If you are experiencing an interruption, it is because the check didn't clear and we are sending out workers to cut the lines. Is there another method of payment you would like to try?" I didn't want to end the call on a bad note and wanted to do all I could in order to help my customer.

"No, nothing at all. I will work something out. Thank you ma'am." His voice softened and his tone changed from when we first spoke.

I heard hesitation in his voice and I hit a few keys overriding the disconnection. It was something we rarely did but were able to do it when a payment was indeed in progress.

"Sir, since your payment is on the way to being clear I notified the technicians to cancel that disconnection. You should be all set within a few minutes to a few hours. Is there anything I can do for you?"

"No Taryn. You have truly been a gem. It's my account for my grandma and I don't like for her to be uncomfortable. It's all she really asks for. I thank you and I do apologize for being so abrupt earlier. I've got a lot on my plate," he apologized and I felt sincerity with it. I sensed a connection with him but didn't want to assume.

"Anytime sir and thank you for calling CompuVision. Do have a good day."

I ended the call and took a sip of Coke. I would have had coffee but my mouth was extremely dry. It felt like someone sucked the life out of me but in a good way. Residual butterflies fluttered in the nest of my stomach and my voice floated for the remainder of the day. Never had I had a reaction to someone's voice before. The only person that made me feel that way was Kenton and he was long gone. My own husband couldn't ignite this feeling anymore. After sitting for almost three hours fielding calls, I decided it was time for lunch.

I walked into my kitchen and pulled out the wedgie I had acquired in my ass crack from sitting all morning. I was sweaty just from sitting and working. I promised myself that I was going to take a shower that night. I tended to wait until the morning but I woke up somewhat late and didn't want to miss calls.

Devon paid me no mind in the morning unless he wanted something, which was almost always, but he wasn't trying to make love before work. The most I'd done was give him head before work and he was so violent in making me swallow his cum that I vowed not to do it again anytime soon.

I also needed to call my mother and apologize for the other night and my outburst. I hated to be disrespectful to my mother but sadly, it was my mother that caused, and influenced my mood and horrible self-esteem. What child drinks Slim Fast at ten years old and gets weighed weekly? Me, that's who. My esteem issues have been lingering from way before my husband. People have told me that I need to lose weight but it won't happen until I feel ready and willing to make a change in my life.

I had three more hours and then I had to get myself together for Devon to come home. As I got ready to dial the pizza delivery number my mother's number flashed on the caller ID. She beat me to it. The problem was I was still on the clock and didn't want her mood to fuck up my vibe. I decided to mute my home phone and tossed it to the side. My mother never called me on my cell phone because she knew of my work schedule. With my new work schedule, I had begun to eat junk food now more than ever before.

I grabbed a packet of cupcakes as I waited for the pizza and ran to the bathroom. I had to pee so bad but tried to hold it. It was amazing how much urine I held inside of me even though I hated water. My version of water was filling up the huge cup of Coke or sweet tea with a tray of ice cubes.

Walking towards the computer, I placed my headphones back on and completed my shift with CompuVision. I can't wait to relax with dinner and dessert. Sometimes I wanted to cuddle up with the food and at times had been found with potato chips and chocolate bars under my pillow. They comforted me. More than my husband could ever.

Hours later, I waited for my scheduled delivery of my pizza to arrive. I ordered and paid for it via computer and since I was a regular customer, they knew to knock and drop it on my welcome mat.

KNOCK KNOCK

Twenty minutes later, I opened my door softly and peeked around the corner. I couldn't bear for any of my neighbors to see what they already knew. I was morbidly obese and had a strong obsession with food.

Devon called me and said it was okay that I ordered something as opposed to cooking since he would be working late. That relieved me of having to appear perfect for him. I just wanted to be me for a few more hours.

Taking the pizza box, I sat on the couch. Next to me, I had a three-liter bottle of Coke, my remote, and hot sauce. I was ready for my evening. Picking up a slice of pepperoni pizza, I placed it in my mouth and the steam hit my nose. I pulled back and began to blow it attempting to bite again. The ringing of the phone interrupted my process and I knew exactly who it was without looking at the caller ID.

"Hi Momma. How are you?" I asked pointedly. My mother never asked me how I was but always had something to say. The cordless phone hung lifeless on my shoulder as I tried to maneuver both the pizza and phone without dropping either. Grease from the slice crept its way down my wrist and made its way to my elbow. I rolled my eyes in exasperation and used a napkin to dab up the mess.

"I'm doing much better Taryn. I wanted to know if you were coming to Wednesday service with me. You know Pastor touched on praying ailments away and I want him to pray for you and your demeanor. You are lonely and it's affecting the relationship between you and me as well as the one with you and your husband."

Edith wanted so much for me to be like her other daughters. It just wasn't in my make up.

"No Ma. I had no intention of going. I have work I need to accomplish and besides won't Kenton be there with you as well? I don't need to be where he is. The purpose of a breakup is to be away from the person you have ended the relationship with. I have moved on and married."

"You're not happily married though. You need someone that's going to love you unconditionally," she said beginning another debate about my love life.

"I'm married. I'm committed. Just like you are my mother but you damn sure aren't my mommy. There's a difference. Learn it," I combatted hoping to bring my point home. Her silence told me that I hit a home run.

I was tired of my mother using every chance she got and trying to reunite my ex and me. I was married. Not happily but married nonetheless. I was committed to the craziness that I called my husband.

"I just want you and he to be friends is all. There comes a time when you have to let go and by letting go you become a better person."

"So I should let go and forgive you for being an asshole to me all these years? Do you think that will help us? Will it help our relationship grow?" I got upset once again about their relationship and revealed my pent up feelings about our strained relationship.

"Taryn it's not my fault that Kenton and I are together. It's not my fault that he chose to be here with me as opposed to being there with you. I keep telling him to go home and reconcile but he says you don't want to see him."

"He's right."

"Is that how you feel about me too? Because every time I ask you to come over you decline." Edith was on the verge of whining and it wasn't doing anything but making my patience thin and the pizza cold.

"As a matter of fact it is. You are the reason why I can't seem to move forward in life. You hound me constantly and throw in my face reasons why I am fat and why Kenton isn't here. Maybe if you weren't such a slut he would have seen you as my mother and not new pussy."

My face grew warm in anger and beads of sweat appeared on my forehead. I had reached my brink and was going far over the edge. Frothy white liquid outlined my mouth as I yelled at the phone in disgust. I was the only one in the house as usual at the moment but it was as if I was speaking to someone face to face.

"How could you talk to me like this? I'm your mot..." Edith tried to plead her case but it was too late. She unleashed an eruption that couldn't be corked with words and simmered with sympathy.

"My mother? My mother? You aren't blood to me. You are dead to me. If you were in my face, I'd beat you like a bitch in the street. Do not ever fucking call me again. Leave. Me. Alone!" I ended the call and tossed the phone across the room. Pictures on the wall felt my rage. I tossed glasses, broke dishes, and toppled over the table. When I was done, it looked like a tsunami ran through it and I didn't care that my husband would be home in an hour. I wasn't going to clean up. I was sick of his shit too.

In a blind rage, I grabbed my shoes, keys, and sweater. Before I knew it, I was out the door and out of the house. Neighbors peered through their window and watched me breathe heavily as I walked briskly throughout the neighborhood. They hadn't seen me leave the house in years. My body and my spirit remained an enigma so to see me actually exist as more than "Devon's wife" brought about some reality to them.

The sapphire sky twinkled and the descending sunlight mesmerized me. It had been a while since I took an evening stroll. I hadn't realized that in being a recluse, I was missing a whole world. After about twenty minutes, I slowed my pace and noticed that I had broken a sweat. My appetite was gone also. My mother had taken my appetite along with my self-esteem.

As I walked past stores and houses, I recognized new ones and some old ones that had been there for years. It had been years since I paid attention to my surroundings. Sadly, the world was going on without me knowing and I was missing out on the best years of my life.

There I was worrying about a man that cared not about my feelings or me and life was moving onward. As I walked, I noticed one of the new businesses was a fitness center called Fitness World. I saw people in there getting their life together. They seemed so much at peace. It was as if nothing and no one mattered. I wanted that peace and tranquility.

Watching the people on the treadmill caused my hands to graze my thighs. I wondered if my legs would ever be able to withstand walking or running for such a long period of time. Grabbing the door with my sweaty hand, I pulled the handle and entered. It smelled like Gatorade and sweat.

I didn't know what to make of it but as soon as my mind changed and I was about to turn and walk away, I was approached by a tall mocha colored man. His bald head shone with perspiration and he kept wiping his face with a white towel that was thrown around his neck.

"Welcome to Fitness World. My name is Asher. Can I offer you a tour of the facilities or answer any questions?"

My heart skipped a beat and I felt myself grow dizzy. Maybe it was the fact that I walked several blocks from my house and hadn't done it in a long time. Maybe it was that I left the house in shambles and my husband was due home any minute if he hadn't arrived already. Maybe it was the fact that the man that I spoke to on the phone earlier that had my pussy wet was standing in front of me. He didn't know who I was but I damn sure remembered that voice. He was just as handsome as I pictured him to be.

The effect he had on me was unbelievable and I stood there in awe of him. His presence had me hypnotized. It wasn't until I felt his hand around my waist did I know that I was on the verge of losing consciousness. He truly took my breath away.

"Ma'am please let me get you to a seat so you can compose yourself." The man named Asher's strong hand held my wrist and guided me to a bench a few feet away. He asked the receptionist for a bottle of water and handed it to me. I unknowingly frowned.

Giving me a bottle of water was like an insult. I was rather thirsty so I accepted and opened it slowly. The coolness numbed my fingers and I placed the bottle to my lips. I actually felt refreshed and it almost tasted a bit sweet as it quenched my thirst.

"Thank you. I, I, just wanted to look inside. I didn't want anything." I opened the bottle again and politely sipped it as every word I spoke to this man caused my mouth to feel like sandpaper.

"Well if you need anything I am here. I am a personal trainer and I am here for your needs. Nowadays people are surprised at how little it takes to get motivated. The change begins with you." Asher bent down to tie his shoelace and I spotted the ripples in his shoulders and arms as he completed the simple task.

"How much is it to get started? I've haven't been in a gym in forever but I'd love to start new."

No time like the present to work off some aggression. My mother had pissed me off and thoughts of Kenton made me want to change things. Devon wasn't a positive influence in my life either and the sooner he realized I wasn't affected by him anymore the easier it would be to leave the relationship. They were going to learn that I wasn't one to fuck with. With them out of my life, I had reason and motivation to change my lifestyle and way of thinking.

"Well we have a special going on. It's twenty dollars down and ten dollars every month thereafter. Personal training sessions with me are free for six months with payment paid in full."

I sat on the bench and considered the offer. I wanted to do something for myself for once. My mother set me off to the point of no return and I wanted to prove to her that things would change when I wanted them to. Now was that time.

With determination and perseverance, I would indeed be another woman. I would finally be the person I always wanted to be.

I stood and walked over to the desk and picked up the clipboard. With Asher by my side, I signed up for the gym and promised to bring the first payment for gym and personal training services. A woman of my word, I brought the payment and was dressed in work out gear to begin my transformation.

<u>Pound for Pound</u>

I walked back home and my stomach rumbled. I didn't know if it was from anxiety or from hunger. I noticed that the light was on and I knew that my husband was home. I turned the key in the lock and entered. Nothing had changed from when I left hours earlier. I smelled the faint smell of cigar and entered the living room. Wafts of smoke curled into the air and Devon turned around in the recliner. He had seen the damage.

"Good evening Taryn." He inhaled and out came puffs of smoke from his lips. To the right of him was a glass of Hennessy White. He sipped and swallowed before speaking again to me. I didn't respond. I wanted to gauge his mood.

"I see you've had quite a day here in the house. Nothing was done and you left quite a mess for me to come home to. That wasn't part of the arrangement when we agreed to this job."

I stared at him waiting cautiously for him to make his next move. I stood perfectly still and watched his calculated movements. I placed my keys in my pocket and walked into the kitchen. I grabbed the broom from the closet next to me and started sweeping up the mess that was left.

After a few minutes, my vision was impaired as I was kneeling down. A dark shadow covered me and it was my husband. The entire kitchen was clean from top to bottom. I would still be punished however, just for the principle of the matter.

"Honey is there something you would like for me to make you to eat? I know you've been drinking and likely waiting for me to make something for you. I ran an errand that took longer than I anticipated. I'm sorry." I wanted to feel him out but he wasn't giving me any feedback. Devon's glassy eyes stared through me as if I was a windowpane.

The shadow of my husband loomed over me and I gasped in fright. I smelled the faint smell of the Hennessy that he was drinking. No sooner than I thought to get up and speak did I feel his hand wrapped around the back of my neck. My hand reached up to prevent more damage but the punishment had already begun.

"I leave you to bust my ass while I'm at work. The only thing you are supposed to do is answer the stupid phones for your fake ass job, cook, clean, and sometimes look like a fucking human. You can't even do that. And you wonder why I don't want to sleep with you at night. You act like an animal and look like one.

What was I thinking when I married you? Answer me!"

I didn't know whether it was rhetorical or not so, I attempted to answer the question. I should have remained silent. His hand swiftly grabbed my neck and pushed me up against the wall. My air supply began to cut off slowly and I gasped with flailing arms. My tiny frame was literally being lifted off the ground as he held me inches off the ground with one hand.

"P-Please Devon. I-I'm sorry; I'll do b-better. I p-promise, don't hurt me anymore," I begged him. I prayed that he would let me down and just when I silently said, "amen" in my head, he did. I collapsed in a heap on the floor.

Look what you made me do. Dammit Taryn. You always do this shit to me. You make me lash out at you and hurt you when I try to be nice. You don't like me being nice do you?" He bent down to eye level and stared at me directly in my face. My teeth chattered, as I feared what he would do next.

He slapped me.

Hard.

"Why do you do make me do the things that I do?"

I wanted to climb into the wall but there was no way that I could. Somehow, he would follow me through and hurt me just as he'd done before.

"Devon, please calm down. Let me explain what happened. My mother called and pissed me off. I was so angry that I threw some things around. I wanted to be home and clean up before you got home but time got away from me. I went for a walk. Please forgive me."

His eyes grew small and darker than I'd ever seen. The next thing I saw was a flash of light and excruciating pain. My face swelled up immediately. I grabbed my eye and I felt it growing on my face.

"Devon why?" I cried out to him in pain begging him not to continue the torture. It fell on deaf ears as he grabbed my wrist and pulled me into the kitchen.

"You don't fucking listen! You need to listen and obey me." I couldn't see out of my left eye and the pain was causing me to grow dizzy. Nonetheless, he had me stand at a hot stove and cook him dinner.

And it was done right.

It had to be or else my other eye would have been blackened. I served his food carefully and he ate it silently while drinking another beer and watching television. I sat on a stool in the kitchen and sobbed. My eye was now swollen shut and in order for me to function, I had to do things more slowly than normal.

"Taryn! I'm finished." I don't know how long I sat pondering my life but it was long enough for my husband to finish his dinner. I walked into the living room and took his tray. He placed the empty beer bottle on top of it and stared at my face. It was almost as if he had some sort of empathy. It would soon be a lie as he made his next statement.

"That eye is ugly as shit. You should grow your hair out so it can be covered the next few days. It will leave a mark." He took his eyes off me and resumed watching the television. It was as if my purpose was just to serve him.

"Is there anything else you need from me Devon?" I asked before I turned on my heel and left.

"Yes. Set my bath water. I want to fully relax."

I sucked my teeth and didn't care if he heard me. That night would be the last time he ever put hands on me. I scraped off his trash and washed his dish. I left the kitchen and walked upstairs to our bathroom.

After I begrudgingly set his water and put a few bubbles in it, I sat on the toilet seat. I watched the water fill the tub and the bubbles rise and pop under pressure. I secretly wished that I were a bubble. I wanted to float away and disappear. I stared at the bruises I had on my wrist. They were throbbing and my face reddened. How could I be with someone that called this love? This was torture and quite frankly a health hazard. My thoughts were interrupted by Devon entering the bathroom.

"What are you doing up here? I was calling you."

He already had his towel and washcloth and was stripped down to his boxers. His mood had changed suddenly and he seemed very mellow. I didn't know whether to be frightened or happy with that change.

"I, I was making sure that everything was to your liking. I know how you like your water and don't want you to be displeased with me." I stepped back so he could enter the bathroom but he reached towards me. I jumped back. He looked hurt. I didn't care really. He was the one that caused all of this.

"Taryn, please don't be mad. Join me so I can make you feel good. Let me make it up to you."

My husband stripped down to his boxers and entered the bathtub. Bubbles surrounded his body and I heard him groan in delight. The water was perfect for him it seemed.

"So you're not going to join me?"

Devon beckoned for me to come into the tub. I thought about it but my common sense kicked in. This was the man that just hurt me. He showed no remorse.

"Would you like to listen to some music baby? Some nice, soft music to set the mood?" I asked as I removed my shirt. My breasts billowed over my bra and my nipples grew erect at the thought of what I was about to do.

"And then you will come inside of the tub with your husband?" I saw his face and I grew warm. His smile was so inviting; so loving. I knew better.

"Yes my love. I will join you," I said as I turned on the radio. I held it in my hand to turn the knob to a station that he would enjoy and then I tossed it into the tub. Sparks flew and I watched as volts of electricity coursed through his body. The whites of his eyes lit up and water splashed everywhere. I stepped back to avoid being in the crossfire. Smoke was everywhere. When it was all over, Devon was gone. The sonofabitch died with his eyes open.

Evil usually does.

<u>Weight in Gold</u>

It had been three months since the funeral of my beloved husband, Devon Hardy. Everyone was so sad to see him go.

I wasn't.

At the repass, everyone wanted me to speak on how wonderful he was. I wished I could have shared the same sentiment but I didn't. I still bore some of the bruises that he left me. He wouldn't ever leave me no matter his position in death or life.

I sat and listened to the conversation of some of his co-workers and bosses. Some were smug. Others praised him. A mysterious woman was seen bawling uncontrollably and I wondered how close she was to him. She cried more than I did and I was his wife. She was one of the few that looked like they cared for him.

His co-workers couldn't resist speaking badly about him. That wasn't my problem. I was more concerned about how he was at home. As much as he was a piece of shit, he left me one hundred and fifty thousand dollars from his life insurance. I was grateful especially since the investigation showed that he caused his own accident. I was in the kitchen; it was said, so I didn't know about the accident until after it happened. I didn't question it.

The police saw the bruises and because of it knew right on the spot that I was a battered wife. I was too timid in their opinion to plan his murder. They were right. I mean it simply happened. It wasn't premeditated so I guess it was accidentally on purpose.

My mother was devastated. So much so that Kenton wondered what was going on between Devon and her. I admit I also had to wonder but I soon realized she was more concerned that she would have to be a mother to me. She liked the fact that she was over fifty fucking a thirty something year old man. Whatever made her happy.

After the funeral and the dust settled, I decided that I would get myself together. I had no need to work because things were taken care of. With the way I cleaned constantly, I opened my own business. I called it "Maid to Order" and employed a few men and women to do some neighborhood cleaning. It became lucrative and I enjoyed running the back end of the business without having to actually get my hands dirty.

I did have to get out and meet new clients on a regular basis and I couldn't do it looking like a slob. I went back to the gym and slowly made progress losing fifteen pounds. Today was my personal training session with Asher. It had only been a month and I already felt so much better about myself. Better than I had felt in a long time.

"Six...Five....Four...Three...Two...One. Good job Taryn. You are really making progress. Now come on over here and get on this scale. It's time for your monthly weigh in," Asher said as he gripped my wrist firmly to guide me onto the scale. Ever since he and I talked that fateful night, we remained friends. There was a reason why he was brought into my life but I didn't know the reason just yet.

No matter what, even though he was my trainer, he still treated me like a woman, which

I was, but he treated me like he was *his* woman. That was a little different from my normal experience. I hadn't been put first like that in a while and it definitely felt special.

I stepped on the scale without my shoes on and closed my eyes. My breath stuck in my throat and I anticipated what the scale would read. Asher calibrated the scale and moved the bar from side to side. My eyes opened partially and squinted to see what the numbers would read.

"No peeking. You already know that you've lost a significant amount of weight. The question is how much," Asher said smiling.

He was proud of my progress and determination. When he met me at first, he didn't think I would make it that far but I had proven to be a worthy partner and client. He didn't even think I would show up again after I paid the initial registration fee but I showed up after all the funeral stuff was over and done with. I wanted to make a change and I knew that it had to start within.

"C'mon Asher. I am just so anxious to see my progress. I know you didn't think I was going to come back and begin working out. I saw it in your eyes."

I knew how he felt when I saw him and that was yet another reason to begin my transformation. It was slow but I was already seeing a difference in my legs and waist. My size 32 body was disappearing and I had whittled down to a size 28. Finally, I would be able to wear clothing that enhances my shape as opposed to covering it up.

"And today's weight is 298 down from 304. You have officially entered the 200's. I am so very proud of you. We should celebrate. Let's go for some frozen yogurt!" Asher said giving me a hug and a kiss on the cheek. As he hugged me hard, my breasts were squeezed by his massive pectoral muscles and I felt my nipples grow erect.

"It's Sunday. The store isn't open when we leave here." I stepped down off the scale and grabbed my bottle of water from the weight bench nearby. I remembered the first time he gave me water. I hated it and now I couldn't get enough of it.

"Well I guess that means I have to take you out to dinner. If not, I'd like to cook for you. You know. Show you some recipes in order to maintain healthy living. You are doing well for yourself but any added assistance won't hurt." Asher smiled at me and we both began walking back to the locker rooms. He continued to convince me on why we should go out to dinner.

I listened intently while he made his pitch. I had already made my decision but I wanted him to want me. It had been a minute since someone wanted me and it felt really good. The more time we spent with each other, the more we bonded. We even laughed about how he called my call center job and I assisted him with the cable bill. He never caught on to my voice but I never forgot his. More so, I never forgot how he made me feel.

"I don't know Asher. I was thinking of getting some salad from the supermarket and just relaxing. I have a big day tomorrow and more so this week. I actually want to go shopping for some clothing because I'm slowly finding myself falling out of the ones I have now." I blushed at that last sentence I mentioned and with good reason.

I had fantasized about sex with Asher for weeks and now that I had lost some weight, my confidence level was growing. I knew there was an attraction to me as well. He touched me as if I was the only woman he cared about. I had observed him with other clients and while he was firm with his training, he at times handled me with kid gloves.

"C'mon Taryn. It would be a good way to begin the week. You can plan some meals and we can talk outside of our gym clothes. I know you are an interesting woman. I can tell by your eyes."

My eyes did speak of lust, desire, and love not revealed. I had forgotten how much I enjoyed sex. I also forgot how it felt to be loved. Because of the abuse suffered at the hand of my husband, I stayed far from any potential love interests. Besides, no one loved a fat girl. I couldn't see my feet let alone my pussy. Asher was changing that day by day.

Minute by minute, he caused me to see more of the world through the eyes of love. While it was new, his interest pushed me to the limit and beyond. If someone could love me despite my flaws, then maybe I was worth being loved.

"Okay fine. Let me just go back home and change clothes. I hate being sweaty. What time did you want to come over? Where are we going? I don't want to be too casual." I fidgeted unconsciously. I always did that when I was nervous. I ran my fingers through my short bob that had grown out since Devon's death. I still had thin spots where the hair wouldn't grow back, but all in all, it was healthy. I was happy with my hair growth as well as my growth as a person. I was starting to trust people again.

"What about I just pick up some items and we cook over at your house? Remember I have my clothes in my gym bag. Is that okay?" Asher was determined to show me a good time. My heart kept telling me yes but my mind kept telling me no. After careful consideration and debate, I decided to follow my heart. I had to give someone a chance to do for me.

"Sure. That's fine. I just..." I hesitated and then caught myself. I had to quit thinking so much about things and just go with what my heart felt. You only live once and if that were any indication as to what living felt like I would enjoy it for as long as possible.

"Be right back!"

Running into the women's locker room, I grabbed my gym bag from my locker after putting in the combination on my lock. My hands shook as I moved the numbers ever so slightly. I took a deep breath and walked out of the locker room to Asher. This was more than just dinner. This was the start of something big. Little did I know that he was feeding my addiction for something more.

<u>Unbalanced</u>

When we arrived at my home, I felt awkward. It had been a while since I had anyone, let alone a man inside. I had always opted to live privately. Even my mother didn't come by without an invitation because not only did I not like her, Devon didn't like her around me influencing me negatively. Also, she just wasn't welcome at our home causing strife with her ghetto self. It was only recently that I began to speak to my neighbors and that was only twice when they received my mail accidentally.

"Here we are. This is my home. Pardon the mess. I am in the midst of revamping my contracts and business plan to get new clients."

I placed my gym bag on the floor, walked over to my dining room table, and closed my laptop as I begun shifting things to the side to make room for my guest.

"Very nice. Very cozy. Comfortable much like you. I can see why you like to stay home often. If I had a home like this, I'd never leave." Asher took a look around and smiled. My home had a nice cozy feel to it and I worked hard to create that after Devon died. He ran a militant household and hated any type of mess.

"Thanks. Now, let me get you out of these clothes." I walked away to a linen closet and smirked as I replayed my last sentence. It seemed very suggestive. "You know what I mean."

I smiled as I handed him the towel and washcloth I had just retrieved and we both chuckled. Our fingers touched during the exchange and I pulled back my hand. It was electric. Our connection was spectacular and not to be mistaken for simple lust.

Asher stared me directly in the eyes and watched them glisten. I blushed and beads of sweat appeared on the bridge of my nose. Stepping closer, he placed his hand around my waist pulling me closer to him. He nestled his face in my neck and inhaled deeply. My heart skipped multiple beats. The desire was just too strong but I avoided getting too close right then with him.

"Yeah I know exactly what you mean. You should get dressed as well. When I am done, we will get dinner and talk. I want to get to know more about you," Asher said wiping sweat from my nose with his forefinger and pinched my cheek softly. Heat traveled to my face and he watched as my eyes glazed. The tension between us caused us to be hypnotized.

As if in a magnetic trance, we leaned close and touched noses with eyes closed. Hot breath was felt between us and the room grew silent in anticipation. The tip of our lips touched briefly and we were interrupted by the doorbell.

"Um, I...I have to get that," I said awkwardly trying to get my composure. I hadn't felt like that in a while. My breath was labored and my palms were sweating.

"Right. Yeah. Where's the bathroom?" Asher asked while curiously watching a shadow outside of the door waiting patiently.

"It's down the hall to the left. If you need any more towels, just let me know, and I will leave some for you," I yelled back to him as I walked to the front door. What waited for me on the other side left me speechless.

"Hi there beautiful! I've missed you." It was Kenton, my ex-boyfriend paying me a visit. I was so angry at his presence I didn't know whether to shut the door in his face or let him in so he could quickly leave. No one was allowed to be at my door unannounced.

"Kenton what the fuck are you doing here? Why aren't you home with Edith?" I now referred to my mother by her first name. My personality went through a transformation with the new weight loss that I had. The change was not only external but it was internal as well.

"Taryn you don't miss me? You are looking pretty damn good. *Wow.* I never expected you to lose all that weight. You might want to continue toning up but damn, I'd fuck you if you let me."

As usual, Kenton's mouth wasn't complimentary to me and it was one of the reasons why I became depressed often.

"I miss you like a hoe misses an STD. Please leave my house before I have to call the police. You are trespassing on my property and I didn't ask for you to be here. I knew I shouldn't have opened the fucking door." I attempted to walk away but he grabbed my arm preventing me from leaving.

"I want to talk. Let's talk. We have too much history to let things just fade out like this."

Kenton pulled me close and it was then that I smelled liquor on his breath. Regardless of his drunken state, he kept trying to kiss me and began shoving his tongue down my throat. I bit him and he pushed me to the ground in anger.

"The fuck you do that for, you stupid bitch!" He hovered over me and I cowered in a corner. With his back turned, he didn't see Asher standing behind him.

"What the hell are you doing to her?" were the only words heard before his fist hit Kenton's left jaw. Blood flew onto the carpet and Asher stumbled and fell into a coffee table sitting in the foyer. A vase lost its balance and shattered leaving water all over the floor.

"Oh my God! What are you doing?" My hands covered my mouth. I was shocked at how Asher came out of nowhere protecting me. I surely didn't expect it and it kind of turned me on.

Grabbing my hand, Asher pulled me up and gave me a once over. He wanted to make sure that everything was ok and I wasn't injured. I was fine physically but emotionally I was still traumatized. All the men in my life seemed to take advantage and abuse me in a variety of ways. I was growing tired of it. I was no one's beating stick.

"Who is this clown? He needs to get the hell out now before I finish him off." Asher was ready to service Kenton another ass whipping for how he treated me. I didn't want any problems. I didn't want Kenton in my house either. The quicker he left, the quicker things would get back some normalcy.

"This is my ex-boyfriend. He and I aren't on the best terms. I haven't seen him in about three months and he was surprised to see me look like this. I just want him to go away. I don't want him around."

"Let's wake him up and get him out so there are no more problems. I'm sure he understands now that you want no more of him. If not, he will have to understand." Asher grabbed Kenton by the collar and placed his arm around his shoulder. Asher and I both took Kenton outside and waited for the air to hit him and wake him up.

"Are you okay?" Asher asked me as he surveyed the possible damage that Kenton left me with due to his untimely invasion. Beads of water caught in between the hairs on his chest caused tiny bubbles. I looked and laughed before reaching out to touch them causing them to pop. Asher ran his hand over his chest and the ripples of muscles made me blush.

"Yes I am fine. I just want him to wake up and go home."

At that very moment, Kenton opened his eyes and began focusing his energy on me. The look Asher gave him told him he had better not try anything. He stumbled up and headed towards his car.

"We aren't finished Taryn. Not by a long shot." He then entered the car, started the engine, and veered off. It wouldn't be the last time we saw him but he wouldn't be around for quite a while if it were left up to Asher.

Focusing his attention back on me, Asher held my hand and walked back into the house making sure that I was securely in his care. I was shaken up but I didn't allow it to change my mood too much. I still wanted us to spend time together.

"Are you okay? Do you need anything? How's your shoulder?" Asher began touching me gently in the area where I fell. It was bruised but I was a big girl literally and didn't stress over it.

"Yes I am fine. I'm sorry that you had to experience that. Kenton is my ex-boyfriend and he's just a lot of bullshit. I don't think I am up to dinner tonight. I just wanna take a shower and go to bed."

I collapsed on the couch and placed my head in my hands. I grew frustrated with my life. Every time I felt like I was making progress and taking a step forward, I was reminded of my past in some way, shape, or form.

Asher walked over and sat next to me with his hand over my knee. The attraction between us was undeniable but we clearly didn't know how to handle it. Silence filled the room and was deafening. The clock ticked and it sounded like bombs exploding. The sounds of our hearts echoed and our breathing rhythmically danced together as one inhaled and the other exhaled. It was a well put together symphony and our eyes were the conductors. We both stared into the other's eyes as if in a trance.

I leaned into Asher and our lips were inches from each other. His hand traveled slowly above my hips making its way to my waist. My hand traced his muscular shoulder slowly and my hand quivered as it approached his neck. My heart skipped beats as my eyes closed. His breath caused me to lose myself in the moment. Just then I realized who I was with and what I was doing, I pulled myself back and left Asher kissing air.

"I can't do this. I, I, I need to be alone. I don't care if you stay but you need to be out of my way. I am not good for anyone right now."

I released my hold from Asher and walked away down my dark hallway and disappeared. Asher, confused and hurt, began to follow behind but entered the bathroom instead to shower and visit his inner thoughts. What just happened? He turned on the hot water and let the steam surround him. I heard him removing his clothing and he dropped them to the floor.

Asher Rollins was thirty-something and grew up within the New York City region. He was as a child, a troubled soul. His grandmother was the only thing that kept him sane. When he was sixteen years old, he was arrested, charged, and jailed for gun possession and possession with intent to sell. While incarcerated he developed a love for lifting weights and personal training. Many of the inmates turned to him to begin training their own bodies and he helped them with conditioning.

After being released, with a certificate in physical fitness in tow, he decided to begin to train others and making money from it. Asher took that certification and began classes in college. I knocked at the door when I had to use it and I had a feeling that he was doing nothing under the shower. I was right there at the entrance when he pulled back the curtain and his fingers were pruned from being in there so long. He quickly turned off the shower and grabbed the towel to dry himself. I stared at his chiseled body as the terry cloth towel draped his masculine waist.

"I'm sorry to bother you but I wanted to get myself together for bed and I needed to use the bathroom. Are you staying or leaving?" I stood there staring at him and he stared right back into my eyes.

I was on a roller coaster of emotions and I didn't know what I wanted to do. I wanted him to stay just in case Kenton came back but I would never admit it. I didn't have to.

"Is there something wrong? Why are you so distant now? I thought we were getting closer." Asher rubbed his bald head and I watched his arms flex and his muscles moved in sync with the rest of his body.

"I apologize. After Kenton came through and ruined the vibe, it was just best to cut the night short. I don't want us to get too tied up with each other. The less of my life you know about, the better."

"He's not here. I am and I won't let anything or anyone hurt you. That much I promise. I've seen too many people in my life that I love and care about hurt because of clowns like Kenton. It won't happen on my watch if I can help it."

Asher's eyes grew small as his past flashed in front of his eyes and he began to grow angry inside. His fists became clenched at his sides and I directed my attention to them. He reached out to touch me and I found myself pulling back.

"I think it's just best that we not get personal. That means you need to go. I will see you at the gym this week but aside from that, nothing more. Thank you for helping me tonight. I do appreciate it." I brushed past him and stood in the bathroom. Asher was forced to walk outside of the bathroom door and watch it close in his face.

I turned on the shower while I was fully clothed and sat on the toilet crying. I didn't want to admit to myself that I had potentially tossed away the man that would care for me like no other. I knew he was passionate about finding out if he was the reason why I changed how I felt. He wasn't.

The problem was, once he found that out, he would find out more than he bargained for.

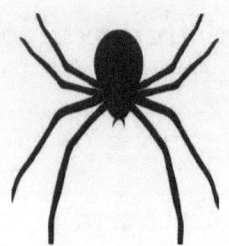

Scales of Justice

Three weeks later and ten pounds gained, I popped the last bottle of Coke that I had in my fridge. I hadn't been back to the gym in almost a month and it showed. I resorted to wearing nothing but sweats again and doing all the things that I shouldn't...including my ex.

It was eight o'clock in the morning and instead of going to the gym, I decided that I would tend to the man that made me feel whole, at least for a little while. As much as I wanted it to be Asher, it was Kenton exiting the bathroom complaining as usual.

"You're out of toilet paper and toothpaste," Kenton screamed from down the hall. He had been there the last week and I regretted every moment of his existence. I was lonely the first two weeks and when the third week approached, I found myself talking to my mother who mentioned that Kenton wanted to see me.

My mouth said no but my heart and body said yes. I regretted it the moment he touched me. All the ill feelings I had came back but now that he was there, I couldn't get rid of him. He was like a scab. I picked it off and threw it away but another one grew covering the old wound.

I didn't want him but I felt comfortable with him being there because he knew who I was and professed his love to me despite my weight. After what happened, he apologized and said he was drunk and wouldn't ever do that again. I wanted to believe him simply because he was genuine in his actions at the time. Now, it seemed that it was a setup and I, of course, would be the fall guy.

"I will get some this afternoon when I go to my meeting. Are you staying or going? Momma has been calling for days and I've been lying to her that I haven't seen you after you got here Sunday. It is now Wednesday so when are you going back? Why did you tell her that you were on a business trip knowing that she would ask? I don't care about the affairs of y'all relationship." I checked myself in the mirror once more.

Since ending the friendship with Asher, I had gained weight and lost all that I was striving towards. Having Kenton around did nothing for my weight and everything for my self-esteem. I still felt sexy but not as sexy as I did with Asher. Gaining weight and losing the one person that had my back caused me to be more conscientious about my looks.

The chance I might see Asher didn't help either. I was always worried when I had a meeting outside of the office with a new client that I would see him. I avoided him and even found different routes so I wouldn't drive past the gym.

Kenton walked up behind me and placed his arm around me. I stiffened in his embrace. He wasn't the man I wanted but my heart continued to deny it. My body convinced him otherwise and he tweaked my nipples that stood at attention at his subtle touch.

"No worries, I ain't staying here. After last night when you were tripping I ain't tryna get caught up in your shit. Just make sure that nigga is out of my way when I am around. No matter what you say Taryn. I am, and always will be, a part of you." Kenton brushed his hand across my cheek and stroked it slowly.   My eyes teared up and my eyelashes glistened with water gathered on my lid. I touched the tattoo that I had etched into my breast with Kenton's name. I had forgotten about it until just now. My heart began racing rapidly at the thought of him and how addictive he was. What had I gotten myself into?

"Kenton just make sure you are not here when I get home. I don't want hair or hide of your ass. If my mother calls looking for you, she will know where you've been. I'm tired of the bullshit you both bring."

"Who's gonna love you like I can? That thick neck nigga? No one wants your ass but me. You keep thinking that weight loss is gonna make you happy. You are still a fat bitch and you will never find anyone but me so you are stuck. If it ain't me, you will be fucking your finger Taryn." Kenton grabbed his fitted cap and began walking out the door but not before smacking me squarely on the ass.

The door slammed shut as he left and I collapsed in a heap on the floor. All the gusto I once exhibited went out with Kenton and I wished that I hadn't called him over after Asher left. I had digressed tremendously and there wasn't any way I would be able to recapture the strength I lost. I needed someone to make me feel good and Kenton had a way of making me feel guilty of wanting love.

I had an appointment and in my current state, there was no way I would be able to make it. I would be staying home that day and rescheduling for another time. I couldn't bear to continue through the day feeling anxiety as I did at that moment. I grabbed my phone and called into the office.

"Hello, Jerron? Yes, it's Taryn. I won't be in the office today but I will be mobile if necessary. Please reschedule all my appointments for the rest of this week. I think I have a stomach virus or something. No, everything is okay. I'm just at the doctor and he's taking forever. I will see you next week. Thanks." I ended the phone call and plopped down on the couch. Piles of clothes tumbled to the ground in a heap.

I looked at the pile of clothes that I could wear and the pile of clothes that I no longer wore. One pile was larger than the other was. Next to the largest pile was a photo frame with a picture of Kenton, my mother, and I. I should have known that there was something between them. Their eyes spoke silently the desire they had for one another. I was oblivious to the impending betrayal. As much as I wanted things to be as they once were, I knew that the life I once led wasn't beneficial for who I was growing to be.

I traveled upstairs to climb into bed. I wasn't feeling up to it today. I just wanted to be held and cuddled. I wanted to hear that things would be okay and I would be the person everyone wanted me to be- STRONG. I wasn't as strong as people perceived.

As I looked at my bed, it was covered with clothing and food. I usually slept on the couch but since Kenton wanted to fuck, we just moved things to the other side of the bed. He never complained and I never changed.

With Asher, it was different. I wanted to be a different kind of woman for him. I wanted to be a different kind of woman for myself. Being around Asher, I was inspired to lose weight and get healthy so I could live a happy life. Now that I had pushed him away I didn't know what happy was anymore. The inspiration left while the weight stayed behind.

"The fuck you in here weeping about? I know you not crying over that sour ass nigga. Bitch you are soft as fuck. I don't know why I bother with your punk ass. Go eat some cake or something. Then come suck my dick. Your mouth needs to be occupied with something and I need to cum before I go to your mother's house. No one can suck dick like you." Kenton had come back into the house and made demands for me to satisfy him sexually.

I looked at him in disgust. I knew then that I didn't want him and he was no better than Devon. I wanted Asher but I knew I treated him horribly ruining the chance that he would ever want to see me again.

"Kenton, why are you still here? I thought you said you were leaving? Go to Momma. You aren't welcome here."

"Bitch you do know that I give you shit so I'm entitled. Don't think that you get shit for free. You gotta work for it," he said grabbing me and pushing me squarely up against the wall.

He stuck his thick fingers inside of my pants and tickled my clit. It burned as the pressure was applied and I inhaled to get my bearings. I wasn't aroused nor was I willing. All I could do was begin to resist but he grabbed me by the wrists and held both hands above my head. His face buried in my neck and his breath reeked of alcohol. He had been drinking yet again.

"Kenton you do know this is my house. You are aware that you can go the fuck wherever you want but you can't come here making demands on shit. I don't belong to you!"

Kenton held me close and pushed me down on the bed while looking into my eyes seductively. I crumpled under his weight and whimpered. He was going to take what he wanted despite me fighting against him. My heart had loved him at one time but the abuse I endured by his hand and by my mother's words was too much to take. Realizing that I deserved better from everyone including myself, I knew that I had enough and began to fight back.

"Please don't Kenton. I will do whatever you say." My voice softened and I begged him to stop as I wiggled under him. The more I fought, the more he tightened his grip around my wrists. Using his massive hand to palm both of my hands to keep me from moving, he used his free hand to undo his belt buckle and pull out his dick. He was moving full steam ahead with his decision to have sex with me whether I consented or not.

"Now, now, Taryn. You know when you tell me no, I get turned on more. I love it when you beg me." With one fell swoop, he snatched off my panties bruising my thighs and leaving elastic hanging from fabric on what was my undergarments. He sniffed it heavily and opened it to the crotch. My moisture lingered and he felt it on his fingers.

Bringing his tongue to the center he licked the material and sucked the middle of the fabric with his eyes closed. Disgusted and frightened, I lay there with my eyes bulging not knowing what to do next. I began to silently pray that he would come to his senses but the way things were progressing, I knew it was almost too late.

"I love it when you cum for me. I'm going to fuck you until you bleed."

Kenton took the tip of his dick and rubbed it up against my clit. I squirmed at the feeling. I hated when he did that because he teased me right before sex with me. It was something that we did regularly. I didn't want to be turned on but I was. I didn't love him anymore but I did love how he fucked me. The issue was that he also verbally abused me as well.

Being around my mother, caused him to take full advantage of me and disrespect me when he saw fit, just like Momma did. Because of my poor self-esteem, he loved making me feel less than beautiful. Asher loved making me feel sexy and wanted. It was what I yearned for all of my life. I didn't realize until I began the process of loving myself.

"Bitch are you listening to me?" Kenton entered my canal and shook me out of my thoughts. I had zoned out briefly but was brought back and decided to regain my life back. In order to do that, I would have to play his game. I would have to pretend that I loved everything he was doing to me.

"Yes Kenton. I was just so lost in how good you feel. Your dick curves to my pussy. It always has. You see how wet and tight you make me. Only you can make me cum like that.

Taste for yourself how you make me feel."
Kenton felt me move my hand and he let go of
it.

Cautious, but still holding me hostage he
allowed my free hand to move southward
invading my pussy hole. My hand massaged my
pearl and I moaned beneath him. It was
working and I felt his dick get harder inside of
me. I slid it out slowly and then he rammed me
once more causing me to gasp. I dipped my two
fingers inside of my tunnel and coated the tip of
my middle finger with the syrupy sweetness. I
couldn't help but cum as I finger-fucked myself
while he was still inside of me.

"Damn ma. You're really messing with my head now. This might not be the last time we fuck if you keep doing this."

"Even if it is, I want you to remember this moment forever." I placed my juices on my lips and pulled his face close to mine so he could kiss me. His tongue lapped up my nectar and he finished it off by biting my bottom lip drawing blood. The mixture of my cum and lifeline caused him to bust inside of me. I suddenly felt a gush of his babies swim within me and I pulled back.

"Baby, you are so fucking big. I love it when you cum in me. You know you last longer when we use condoms. Let me get one from the side table and put it on for you." Realizing that I was no longer fighting the moment, Kenton eased up on the restrictions and let me seduce him.

"You got me thirsty as fuck. I can't wait to really give it to you." Kenton eyed a bottle of Hennessy on the other side of the bed. We had been drinking it the night before. "Pass that shit to me so I can feel nicer than I've been feeling," he said massaging his dick.

"Whatever you want baby," I said as I passed him the bottle of Hennessy. The next thing you heard was gulps echoing in the room as cool liquid rushed down his throat. He finished the bottle and passed it back to me as the liquor affected his speech. Every word was now slurred and his balance was off. He was already drunk and that just made it worse.

"You are a nasty, sloppy, worthless bitch and no one is gonna love you but me. This pussy right here is mine ya heard." He knelt down whispering his hot breath into my face. I grew tired of the verbal bullying and as I was placing the bottle back on the dresser, I decided to utilize his momentary lapse in judgment to my advantage.

Without warning, I brought the bottle back up and smashed the bottle upside Kenton's head leaving shards of glass in his skull as a reminder of his invasion. He pulled out of me and I watched him stumble back off the bed collapsing and grabbing his head as crimson fluid oozed rapidly amongst his fingers.

"You bitch! What the fuck are you doing?" Kenton screamed in horror. He was taken aback by my violence but I wasn't done yet. He fell on his back and soon I was the aggressor. I stood over him and knelt at his side. Not to be outdone, and sick and tired of being called out of my name, I scoured the bed for a weapon. I found a triangular piece of glass from the broken bottle and held it gingerly in my hand. It was sharp and jagged as it sat in my hand.

"I am tired of you calling me out of my name. You are nothing but the devil and I fucking hate you." I straddled him and tears from my eyes fell onto his chest. I didn't care anymore. I wanted him to know that I would be in control from now on.

I closed my eyes and pierced Kenton's throat preventing him from screaming. He forgot about his bleeding skull and focused his attention on his neck, which was gushing blood. His voice box was now damaged and crying for help was futile.

As blood trickled down Kenton's neck, there was a gurgling sound as I took the make shift knife and punctured his throat severing his artery. There was nothing he could do but beg for mercy with his eyes, as his mouth was no longer an option. I watched the life drain out of him and he reached out to me for help. His fingers stained with his own blood grabbed my clothing and left red prints but I swatted him away.

In a daze, I stared at him and watched my ex-boyfriend expire in front of my eyes. I was in shock at what just happened and heard a voice behind me. Someone was in the house and might have seen or heard what just went down. I got up, put a pair of sweats on, and tossed a heap of clothes over the corpse. I needed to see who the visitor was. Blood stained my tee shirt and I forgot to remove it. Surely, questions would need to be answered but depending on who it was, they could meet the same fate as Kenton.

Karma

I stood in the pitch-black hallway of my apartment and watched the figure creep with catlike motions into the foyer. I wiped my bloodstained hands on my thighs and held the homemade weapon of glass in my left hand. I didn't mean to kill Kenton but he was getting exactly what he deserved. The door creaked open and the figure stepped through.

"Taryn? Are you home? The door was left open!" I heard my name called and looked to see me mother.

"What the hell are you doing here? You know you could have gotten your ass killed?" Ironically, I had forgotten that I had a murder weapon in my hand.

"I wanted to come and see how you were. I hadn't heard from you in weeks. You are still my child despite not wanting to have anything to do with me. Why are you hidden in the shadows? Taryn you are scaring me. You know I am having trouble walking due to my weight. My heart can't take it."

"All the more reason for you to have stayed your ass at home Momma. I won't be responsible for anything that happens. You brought it all on yourself"

Anger rose up inside of me and I gripped the glass feeling a burning sensation as it punctured my palm. Blood dripped down my wrist and onto the floor leaving ruby spots onto the wood. I would have to handle that later but for now, I had to get my mother out of the house. The question would it be dead or alive.

Edith hobbled with little balance towards the darkness. I heard her inhale slowly. It was as if she smelled the death in the air. With her torrid past, she knew what it was and her senses perked up. Wearing flip-flops, and sweat pants coupled with an oversized tee shirt, she approached me carefully and with good reason. She knew in the past that I had behavioral problems and wondered when they would come to light.

It was only a matter of time before I sought out my revenge for her stealing my boyfriend and for making me feel like shit for many years. People can only make you feel like shit if you allow it but because she was my mother, I had no choice but to believe her opinion of me.

"Taryn I just want to make sure you are ok. I know things have been rough for you but they have been rough for me too. I haven't seen Kenton in a while. I know he's been with you. I've smelled him when he comes by. He doesn't want me to tell you. It's okay though. I stole him from you and you stole him right back. He belongs to no one honestly. You are my daughter. You should have come first."

"Momma I don't want to hear any apologies. None! You betrayed me and I don't care anymore. You turned me into the woman I am." I wiped my face and left a bloody smear mark on my right cheek. It was then that the emotions began pouring out of me like a broken dam. I began to cry uncontrollably at what had become my life.

"Taryn I'm sorry. You are beautiful. You are mine. No one can love you more than me," Edith said; words that struck me like a Mack truck.

Edith didn't know what love was. She was having sex with my boyfriend, Kenton, like it was okay. That hurt me to the core. There were times when she even convinced me to engage in threesomes with them. I did what I felt I needed to do to nurture the relationship I had with my mother and my man. With both of them out of my life, it didn't matter anymore.

Stepping out of the shadows, I looked directly at my mother who was stunned at my appearance. Slowly I walked to her and stared her directly in the eyes. Tears welled up in them as I saw nothing but a mirror image of the person that I once was. Overweight, miserable, and void of what real love is.

"Love? You know nothing about what love is. You will never know what love is. I loved you because you were my mother and was forced to respect you even though you deserved none of it. The things I did were to have you love me but you failed to realize it. You belittled me every chance you got. I had love and I lost it. I lost the love I had for myself. Devon treated me like shit because I allowed you to treat me like shit. I won't allow it anymore." I walked closer and closer to her and with every word spoken, the veins popped out in my neck and forehead.

"I, I, don't know what to say." Edith stumbled back into a wall and stared at me. I was the child that she birthed but in that moment, she realized that I had become a stranger. The realization was that she had created a monster that could no longer be tamed.

"There's nothing to say Momma. I love you. I always did and always will." I placed my hand around my mother's neck and embraced her. I pulled back and looked into my mother's eyes. I kissed her left eyelid and then her right one. Tears crept out of them and landed on her cheek.

As the tears fell, I reached over and kissed them slowly. I licked my mother's tears and made my way to her lips. Parting them slowly I slipped my tongue into my mother's mouth with a French kiss. I held her close while allowing my tongue to roam aimlessly as if searching for something.

We stood in the foyer like long lost lovers and kissed as if it was the last time we would see each other. My pussy creamed with feelings of arousal. That was the third time I felt that and the adrenalin rush was overwhelming.

The first time was when I killed Devon, and just recently, when I killed Kenton.

Without warning, there was a gasp. Eyes rolled in the back of the head and there were sounds of gurgling and searching for air. Hands clamored down my back and I held up the dying body of my mother. The one that gave me life was now begging for hers to remain. Life was escaping slowly and I whispered into my mother's ears for the last time before I let her drop.

"Shhhh Momma. I said I would always love you. I love you like Judas loved Jesus and we all know how that turned out"

#####

Asher spent weeks at the gym waiting on Taryn to appear but she never did. He was tired of waiting for a love that wasn't reciprocated.

"Yo my man, you ready to lock up?" an employee asked tossing the keys to Asher as he replaced the weights and completed his last client for the evening. He loved the changes that he was responsible for but it was all them. He wished that Taryn would change her mind about them but that was something he would have to adapt to.

"Yeah I'm good. Thanks and I will see you tomorrow afternoon." Asher caught the keys and placed them in his pocket as he continued. As he cleaned up and

locked up the fitness center for the day, he thought about Taryn. He wanted to know how she was doing with her regimen and if she thought about him too.

No other woman had an effect on him like that and they hadn't kissed nor had sex. He definitely didn't stress over sex. He wasn't interested in it randomly. Since being home from prison, he had fucked a few women but it was nothing that he wanted to call an exclusive relationship. It was all about momentary sexual gratification. The connection that transpired between them was nothing like the one he had with Taryn.

Asher locked up the gym and tossed the keys into his bag. He removed his car keys and walked slowly towards the car. He smelled the air, which was scented

with freshly fallen rain. That reminded him of Taryn. She

loved the rain and refused to run in it for fear that her

clothes would get soaked. He chuckled at the thought

that men believed that black women didn't work out for

fear that they would ruin their permed hair. Taryn

wasn't that woman. She loved to work out once he was

able to find an exercise regimen and stick to it to help her

meet her weight loss goal.

Sitting at a stop light, he wondered if she would

be freaked out by a visit even though they had not seen

each other in weeks. He wasn't even sure if she would

welcome it. If he made a left, he would be able to casually

cruise by the house without too much of a problem if

caught. If he made a right, he would be out of his way and she would definitely believe that he was stalking her. After debating the options, he decided to follow his heart and drove casually by her apartment. What he saw caused him to slow the car to a screeching halt.

<u>Oversized</u>

amn this bitch is fat and sloppy," I said as I hauled my mother's heavy corpse and wrapped it as best as I could in a carpet that I had laid out. It was the biggest that I could find but I had intentions to get rid of it anyway. It was one of the few things that I had left from Devon. Using some twine, I rolled up the body and tied it closed. My neighbor was supposed to help me get rid of the carpet but never responded. The carpet needed to go and now was as good a time as any.

I thought to myself that it was good that I was working out because it took all of me energy to haul and pull my mother's dead weight out of the house. Even though I hadn't been to the gym in a while, I still maintained my muscle tone, which I needed to drag the corpse through the front door. I dragged the body wrapped in carpet to the front door and left it there. I then walked out towards my truck that was sitting in the front driveway. I patted my pockets and realized I had forgotten my keys. I walked back into the house and grabbed them off the table located in the foyer.

The mahogany wood was stained with blood. It was yet another item that would have to be removed or be void of evidence that a murder, no, two took place that day. As I had my keys in my hand and opened my front door, I stumbled upon my nosy neighbor Chemira.

Chemira was my neighbor for the past three years and she was one of those people that used to ostracize and insult me. She knew that Devon was having an affair yet she didn't say anything. I found out at the funeral when a mysterious woman approached me giving condolences. It honestly didn't matter to me. What was done was done.

My neighbor hadn't spoken to me in months yet today of all days she wanted to maintain a conversation with me. I hated speaking to people that were sometimey. The only reason she wanted to talk to me was because she saw me leaving the house and she noticed my weight loss. If she only knew that I held grudges like a muthafucka and revenge was imminent.

On that particular day, Chemira wanted to know what was going on as she heard a lot commotion inside of the house. She decided however to wait until she felt the coast was clear before stepping into something that might have very well imploded in her face.

I noticed her peek from across the street as she picked up her mail from the mailbox. She wanted to know what I was doing, who I was doing it with, when, were, and why. I would give her all the info she needed and she would soon become an accessory and victim without even knowing.

Chemira was light skinned with hair that was jet black and she had hazel eyes. She was the type woman that the authors in the books I read always describe their leading ladies to be. No one looked like me. I hated that sometimes and that helped with my body issues. I was brown skinned and fat. My husband hated how I looked and my dream was to have him love me.

He lusted after her often when he was alive and I loathed watching her saunter past him when she saw him. She didn't need to work out on the front lawn when it was hot, yet she did her splits and stretches with her ass cheeks hanging out so he could see.

Her body resembled Deelishis from "Flavor of Love" and she felt that all men wanted to get between her legs. They did and she was right, but what she was mistaken about was that they didn't want me as well. They were quicker to be attracted to me because I carried myself like a woman of character. Well I did until crossed.

Chemira peeked her head out of the door after seeing activity outside of her home and being the nosy woman she was, she wanted to investigate and see what all the ruckus was about.

Chemira walked out of the apartment and casually decided it was time to check the mail. In full diva form, she sashayed her fat ass down the block to antagonize her rival. What she didn't know or realize was that she was in the wrong place at the wrong time.

"Taryn what are you doing? You should be having some sort of garage sale if you're gonna get rid of all that stuff. Can you even manage it by yourself?"

Chemira stood by the mailbox in her denim booty shorts showcasing her tramp stamp tattoo located above her ass crack. Many people drove by and watched her pick at her stiletto shaped fingernails while she snapped her bubble gum rhythmically. She clearly wanted to piss me off by making herself the center of attention.

She was helping unbeknownst to her, because no one noticed me or my activities anymore, which worked in my favor. I decided to humor the chick that was working my nerves because sooner or later she would cause a scene and the last person that did that wasn't on this earth anymore.

"Chemira, I am finally cleaning up my house and getting rid of the fucking garbage. One never knows how much shit we accumulate but finally I decided now was the best time to clean up and move on. It feels so good."

I wiped the sweat that almost escaped from my forehead into my eyes and I proceeded back into the house. I had dragged the carpet containing my dead mother right near the door and begun the process of discarding of the body. I walked back to the front door and saw Chemira still standing there watching me break a sweat as she casually stood there. Her presence had begun to annoy me.

"Bitch you sure have a lot to say. You wanna help or is your main purpose to just stand there looking cute?"

I wanted Chemira to either stay there and continue to distract or she could leave. Either way, she needed to figure out her purpose or leave because I was on a mission and still had Kenton to discard. I never knew murder involved such cardio.

"Oh jeesh. You tend to be so mean to me. I just wanted to ask you where that cute little boyfriend of yours was. He hasn't been around here today. Not that I've seen. Your home is like a fucking roach motel. People check in but they don't check out." Chemira blew a large bubble with her gum and it popped so she took her finger and wound it around her digit placing the gum back into her mouth.

I laughed to myself at that last comment. I looked at Chemira squarely in the eyes and whispered with purpose and intent. I wanted her to fully understand what was happening.

"Sometimes one must get rid of the shit that weighs us down in order to move on...people included," I said and laughed as I walked past Chemira.

Chemira didn't know how to take that and popped her gum. Her ebony hair lay on her shoulders and she pushed a stray piece behind her ear. Shifting the weight from her left leg to her right, she glanced down at her flip-flops to see ants gathering at her feet. She stomped them looking bored and not knowing what to do. I looked up at her and rolled my eyes.

"Are you gonna just stand there and do nothing? Make yourself fucking useful or go the hell home Chemira. I've got more stuff to get out of the house."

I brushed past her once more and began hauling the multi-colored carpet to my car. Holding it carefully to avoid a body part from sticking out, I dragged it inch by inch. Chemira never noticed that I wore black gloves and blood stains. She grabbed the carpet just as I was coming back with it and helped me hoist it into the car.

"Damn this carpet is heavy," she said grabbing the middle and hoisting it up above her waist. It was the best she could do but it was much more help than I had before. I would have had to get rid of the body alone and now with Chemira's fingerprints, the evidence could point to her.

"Yeah, it's one of those foreign fabrics that weigh an arm and a leg literally. I'm redecorating so I don't need nor want it anymore. I've got another one in there as well from my bedroom. This is from my living room,"

I explained as we both grunted and groaned under the weight of Edith's carpeted body.

Hoisting it up in the air, we were able to get it in the back seat of my truck. I watched Chemira shut the door on Edith's hand that peeked out of a piece of the carpet. Her pointer finger severed and landed on the sidewalk without her noticing. I did and gasped bringing unwanted attention to myself inadvertently.

"SHIT!"

"What's wrong? You didn't want it in the back seat?" Chemira grew confused and wanted to be as helpful as possible if she was to gain my trust.

"Oh, nothing. I just had a horrible pain in my side. And to think, I've gotta do the other carpet as well. I'm tired." I walked back into the house to get the other carpet containing Kenton's body and leaned up against the wall of my foyer and adjusted my gloves. I was exhausted and I chuckled to myself knowing that Chemira's help was appreciated and I would keep her around for as long as possible....Until...

Calibration

had no idea that Asher was watching me until I saw his car out of the corner of my eye. It had been a while since I'd seen him but I had been looking for his car so often that seeing it when I didn't expect it caught my eye.

I saw as he watched me and Chemira move the carpet out of the house and place it in my backseat. My goal was to remove things that no longer benefitted me much like my mother Edith, my husband Devon, and my ex-boyfriend Kenton.

Asher drove up past the house and I smiled. I felt my skin grow warm as he parked the car behind my truck and opened the door. His biceps curved and curled with every movement causing my nether regions to react with arousal. I watched him walk towards me as I closed the car door.

Chemira lingered nearby and stood on one leg as she chewed her gum. She stared at Asher lustfully adjusting her top and clearing her throat waiting for an introduction.

Stepping out of the car, he walked up the driveway. I watched him survey the situation and his eyes glanced upon the car, which upon further inspection, I saw that he noticed the hand sticking out of the car door. Asher jumped back and almost fell to the pavement.

I noticed a concerned look on his face. He wiped his hands on his pants as they excreted perspiration due to nerves. His breath grew shallow and his stance told me that he activated his fight or flight mechanism. This was something that needed to be explained.

"Asher, what are you doing here?" I asked as I approached him and ended up walking smack dab into his muscular chest. His scent tickled my nostrils and I grew aroused due to nostalgia. I took my keys out of my pocket to take the carpet to the junk yard and then return to finish my clean up. Chemira walked up behind me and stared at the new accomplice. She had offered to ride shotgun but would gladly hang out in the backseat if she needed to.

I stood back and contemplated my current situation. I had two dead bodies to get rid of and I also had my crush and my nosy neighbor in tow. One or both of them would have to go. I couldn't risk either of them discovering my secrets and telling the police.

I grew worried that Asher was there; it would either hurt or help the situation. How much did he know? How much did he see? I surveyed the area and realized that he might know more than he let on which meant that as much as I cared for him, I would have to kill his ass too.

"Asher you are just in time. I'm sorry I've missed our personal training sessions. I just have been feeling so unlike myself lately. I miss you though." I walked over to him and traced his triceps with my finger and placed my hand around his waist. Chemira grew jealous and began to compete. She eased over to his other side and placed her hand on his chest.

"Oooh a personal trainer! I need some training personally and I think you are just the man for the job. I need a reason to break a sweat," Chemira flirted incessantly but Asher paid no attention to her.

"How about we take this stuff to the dump, get cleaned up, and all go out to dinner. I need to clear my head and a drink or two would definitely help. You down?" I looked right at Asher for a response but Chemira's mouth spoke for both of them as if they were one.

"We would love to. Let's hurry up so we can come back" Chemira walked over to the truck and hopped in. She left the door open for Asher to join her in the front seat.

"Let's just get this out of the way. You and I definitely have things to talk about but we can't do it with her around. She's gotta get out of here." Asher touched my shoulder and whispered to me.

His touch made my pussy leak. Goosebumps formed on my arm and I wanted him right then and there. It was amazing how a single moment transformed me into a creature that the world wouldn't be ready to tame. Moments later, with everyone in the car, we drove twenty minutes to the dump and rid ourselves of the bodies that I, Taryn, single-handedly killed.

Three Strikes

riving back in the car, we were all silent and tired. No one knew what to say. Chemira was pissed that Asher was talking more to me than her and Asher wanted to talk to me but didn't know how to and where to begin.

Once we traveled back to my house, we sat for a minute. I couldn't take the silence so I decided to speak. Everyone took spots on my sofa and loveseat as we thought about next steps.

"So y'all decide what to do? I'm hungry as shit and y'all ain't helping me none. I'm gonna go take a shower. Mira, please stop throwing your pussy at Asher. I beg of you. Asher, you and I will talk, I promise."

I disappeared down the hallway and grabbed a towel to shower. I entered the bathroom and turned on the faucet. The hot water blared through the pipes and the bathroom mirror steamed up as I removed my clothing. As I was about to step into the shower, I wiped the steam away and saw a reflection of my mother.

"They're gonna find out about you and me. Nothing from the dead remains buried," the voice spoke through the glass.

I turned around and saw nothing. *Eerie,* I thought and continued to step into the shower. I remained in the bathroom to get rid of the dirt and blood from my victims and when I emerged from the bathroom, I traveled to my bedroom. Since we were going out, I decided to get something to wear to dinner. No matter how I felt, I was a woman of my word and a little integrity especially since they helped rid me of the baggage I had.

"Did you stay in there so I could get tired and leave?" a voice called out from the darkness.

He blended in so well that he couldn't be seen amongst the shadows. Asher sat in the dark on my bed and I had no idea.

"What the fuck are you doing in here? I thought you left. I, I wanted you and I to have a private moment." I was at a loss for words and fiddled with my towel that swaddled my wet skin. Trails of my footprints led from the bathroom to the bedroom.

"I get the feeling that you are avoiding me. It's almost like you are hiding something from me. What is it?" Asher spoke from the darkness. I reached over and turned on a lamp and he watched me while crossing his legs waiting for a response.

"What do I have to hide? I just have been dealing with my ex-boyfriend. It was a long day. I'm tired and I want to relax. I care about you and I want us to be more than friends. I'm scared of loving you. It might not be enough. I might not be enough. I realized after I left just how much I love you."

I walked over to him and placed my hand on his face. Asher touched my wrist and kissed the inside of it. His lips traced the welts on the underside that told the brief tale of when I didn't love myself enough. Getting up off the bed, he turned on the lamp on the nightstand.

"What happened to your hand? It's bruised and swollen. Taryn something happened here and I know it. You changed into a different person and I don't know who you are anymore."

I released myself from Asher's grip and dropped my towel. Standing there in my nudity, I watched his reaction as the light radiated against my skin. My stretch marks looked like small tattooed lines against my expresso colored flesh.

"Here I am, exposed to you. There's nothing more than what you see and nothing less than what I've given you."

Asher walked over and touched my shoulder ever so slightly. My breasts reacted to his touch and my nipples grew erect. The areolas that decorated my breasts favored chocolate circles and the nipples resembled chocolate kisses.

"You've not given me everything. I want to know what's in your heart. You shed your insecurities and your weight but you still have some resentment towards someone or something. Don't let it be the reason we don't work out." He slowly breathed onto my lips and kissed me slowly as if giving me life. I slipped my tongue into his and we let passion take over.

Asher picked me up and carried me to the bed. He removed his shirt and held me close to his chest while I played with his nipple. He was very sensitive and began moaning as my hot tongue flickered onto his skin.

"Asher I don't know if we should. Isn't Chemira in the next room? She will hear us." I caught myself from the throes of my passion and realized what was happening. I fought furiously to try to free myself from his grasp but was unable to. He leaned on top of me and kissed me full on the mouth.

"I've wanted you from the moment I saw you. The funny thing was we knew of each other before we knew each other. Did you ever think you would hear my voice and then I would be this close to you?" Asher slowly removed the towel from my body and traced his tongue up my shoulder kissing my neck. I tensed up and gripped his naked back leaving fingerprints.

"I, I want you but I'm scared. I don't want to get hurt." Tears escaped from my eyes and he leaned over kissing them away.

"No one can hurt you unless you allow it and I'm here to protect you as best as I can. Keep your guard up and your heart pure. I can only promise to love you. The rest consists of allowing me to love you the way you need to be loved."

He wiped a stray hair away from my face and buried his face into my breasts listening to my accelerated heartbeat. It beat like the rhythmic sounds of African drums. I didn't know how to control how I felt around him. He brought out such passion inside of me and took my breath away. I couldn't control myself around him, which was why I ran from him, and the feelings that I had regarding him.

During that moment, I realized that I wanted more than just sex with him. This man had stripped me of my fear. Abandonment wasn't an issue anymore. I would keep him around even though the arousal grew to kill him.

My pussy was on fire with each touch he placed on my body and I fought the urges. No longer was I addicted to food. I loved to kill and maim and that's what made me feel good. Sadly, it was usually the ones that I loved that became my victims.

That was why I didn't want to love Asher, because sooner than later he would succumb to the same fate. Asher placed his hard dick inside of me and I gasped in amazement as the feeling took me out of my current thoughts. My pussy enveloped it as if it was a missing piece of a puzzle. He moaned in ecstasy and my body glided beneath his as we both moved in motion like waves of the sea.

"Shit, you feel so good." Asher grabbed my waist and dug deeper within me as if to capture my soul. He kissed my shoulder blade, neck, and lips one at a time.

Tears began to well up in my eyes and I looked away from him. It had been a long time since a man paid me that much attention. I was truly being made love to and it was a wonderful feeling. Asher noticed my tears and moved a wisp of hair from my face.

"You want me to stop? I can if you want me to. You seem uncomfortable." Asher stroked my skin slowly and pinched my nipples causing electric shocks to course through my body. He knew I loved the feeling that he was giving but wanted to hear me say it.

"N-N-No, please don't go. I-I I need you to stay. I need you to cum with me. I need you to l-love me." I barely got the words out. I felt I needed no one. I hated needing Devon and I hated needing Kenton. Neither of them worked out and my mother taught me not to depend on anyone.

Music softly played in the background and "So Beautiful" came on causing Asher to stare at the radio. He looked down at me and kissed me slowly biting my bottom lip.

"Girl don't you know you're so beautiful? I wanna give all my love to you girl. Not just a night, but also the rest of your life. I wanna be always here by your side"

He sung the words to me and a hot teardrop escaped from my eyes landing in my ear. I wiped it away and he kissed my eyelid.

"Don't make it seem like you will be here forever. I know your type." I moved my face away and retorted almost in anger. I didn't want him to know how good he made me feel.

Asher began making love to me again but this time harder. With each stroke, he grew more determined to bring me to climax and give of myself. Harder and harder, he pounded into my pussy until I was rendered speechless. I couldn't articulate anything other than guttural moans of pleasure. He had me right where he wanted me.

As I felt him in and out of me rhythmically moving within my spirit and body as if he was owning me. I was in another world. I didn't even notice that Chemira stood open mouthed in the doorway. I saw the lust in her eyes before Asher did.

"Uh uh, tell me you like it. Tell me you want it. I'm putting my name on this shit." Asher pounded furiously as he increased his speed and tossed me around the bed.

Chemira watched this and began to get turned on. She found herself moaning as she watched and I turned my head to watch my neighbor observing my pleasure with her mouth agape. I pointed at her and curled my finger towards her calling her closer to us. Asher noticed that my attention was elsewhere and turned his head as well. His focus was still on me and giving me pleasure.

"Don't be a stranger. Join us."

Asher looked at me and continued claiming my pussy confused at the invitation but embracing it as it is every man's fantasy to have an extra woman in the bedroom.

"I, I didn't mean to interrupt. I just wanted to know what was taking so long. I will leave y'all alone." Chemira walked backwards and almost crashed into the wall.

I sat up and guided myself from underneath Asher. He removed himself from on top of me and sat stroking his erect dick. I sat on the edge of the bed and patted it for Chemira to sit next to me with Asher on the other side.

"The rule is if you come past the threshold, then you can't leave. Anyone that enters my bedroom doesn't ever leave the same." I grinned because I knew that fact was very true. I grew bold and leaned over kissing Chemira on the lips and she pulled back astonished at the move of seduction.

"I need to go. I'm not ready for this." Chemira stood up in front of us and stuttered. She was ready to go but her eyes kept darting back to my breasts and his dick. Her legs were keeping her there even though she wanted to bolt towards the door.

"You wanted to chill with us so now you do what we say. Ain't nothing wrong with a little sharing. Do you mind if we share with her baby?" I turned to Asher and watched him stroke his still hard dick. He loved the exhibit and it aroused him more than he knew it would.

"Nah, I don't mind at all. Y'all can do whatever and I'll just sit here 'til you are ready for me." Asher eyed an ottoman in the corner of the room, grabbed a towel, and sat on it. He knew if he continued he would make a mess and wanted to protect anything that might be in the way.

"So it's settled. It's playtime. I know you want me just as much as I want you. I've been eyeing your sexy ass for months," I said as my hands reached up to began to remove clothing.

First, the shirt was gone. Then the bra was tossed across the room leaving Chemira's honey colored breasts revealed. I laid her down and began to suck on her nipples. Chemira moaned and bit her bottom lip. Soon she felt her panties and her jeans being removed. She was free from restriction. Her shoes were on the floor near the bed.

"You like that shit huh? Good. Because when I'm done with you, you will know what it feels like to die in ecstasy." I leapt down and pried Chemira's legs open to reveal her neatly shaved jewel. I opened it with my fingers and stuck a finger inside getting it wet with her potion.

Removing my finger, I placed my glazed digit inside of Chemira's mouth. I rubbed it all over her lips and then placed it back inside of her tight hole. I removed it once again and looked at Asher as he sat. I watched him stroke his hard dick and saw it dripping onto his thigh. I sucked my finger and licked my lips.

"Damn you taste sweet."

I watched as Chemira's eyes rolled in the back of her head. I gave my attention back to her pussy. I began to lick and suck on her pearl which raised its head beyond the hood. Chemira could no longer withstand the pleasure that she was faced with. I chuckled as I thought of how this situation was taking place.

Everything and everyone was playing their part perfectly even though they threw a monkey wrench in my plan. My bedroom had become the last place many of my victims were seen. Surely, I didn't plan for it to be that way, but at least they left this earth with a smile. I glanced quickly at the bloodstain on the rug that Asher stood on unbeknownst to him.

"Do you love me Asher?" I asked suddenly as I began finger-fucking Chemira and waited for an answer. Asher was a mere man and as much as he wanted to appear as if he was different, the testosterone said otherwise.

"Yes, I do love you. I loved you before I met you," he said as he stroked his balls softly. He sat on the ottoman with a glazed look in his eyes as if he were hypnotized. Technically, he was; he had never experienced the pleasure that I was providing so the stimulation was undeniably arousing.

"Good. That's just what I wanted to hear. I need you to do something for me. Come fuck her. I wanna see your dick pound her 'til she can't take it anymore. Make her beg like I just did."

"Taryn no! I don't want to do it." Chemira began to get up from the bed and exit the room. I pushed her back down and straddled her chest.

"Bitch you were just spread eagle with your clit comfortably sitting on my tongue. Now you wanna act shy because the man that you have been lusting after all day has just been ordered to fuck you? What part of the game is that?"

I placed my hand around her throat and she gasped for air. I reached back and played with her clit. She moaned and I nodded to

Asher to come over to the side of the bed and finish the job. Asher did as he was told.

He grabbed a condom from the nightstand and I took it from him. I opened it and placed it in my mouth. Slowly I placed him inside of my mouth. When I stopped sucking, he was covered with the thin sheath of protection. It was about to go down!

"Get your ass up," I ordered Chemira. She stumbled as she arose but was soon tossed back on the bed and flipped onto her stomach. In one fell swoop, he entered Chemira deep and she couldn't breathe. All she could do was gasp as her pussy was being murdered by Asher's thickness.

"Uh, uh, oh!" Chemira gushed for the first time all over his dick and I smiled at the look on both of their faces.

Never had I seen a woman squirt but it was something that caused me to be turned on a great deal. I was used to licking snatch and being the one doing the squirting. Asher stared at me with impending approval. I smiled at him and he continued. Chemira looked at me with eyes begging me to save her. I wouldn't. She wanted to be involved in our triangle and now she would be whether she changed her mind or not.

I wasn't a stranger to having a third join me in sexual escapades. I had engaged in threesomes with my mother and ex-boyfriend Kenton for years. It wasn't something I was proud of but it happened and I was over it, much like I was over them. It hurt to see them both die but it needed to be done. I was tired of being hurt. I was tired of not being in control and now I was the one calling the shots.

"Fuck her harder!"

"What the fuck did you just tell me to do?" Asher asked me as he noticed for the first time the terror in Chemira's eyes. He was confused as to what I was doing because he thought it was a threesome. It seemed however, that torture was the only thing on my mind for Chemira whose pussy had been pounded.

"I said, I want you to fuck her harder. No one told her to bring her nosy ass over to my house. She wanted to see who you were and if you were fucking me. Now, she's in a position to get fucked." I glared at Chemira in disgust. She knew that she wanted to fuck Asher so this was her perfect opportunity. Unfortunately it wasn't the way she fantasized since he had been coming around.

Asher rolled Chemira's body over and hung her head off of the bed. His body straddled Chemira and her face damn near touched the carpet. I began playing with my pussy and causing electric shocks to course through my body with orgasms. Wet spots covered my bed and I decided to join the fun.

I placed my body underneath Chemira's lips and she had nothing else to do but to lick my pussy. I felt her nose tickling my clit and my nipples hardened. I saw Asher's eyes glaze as he watched me grow aroused and reach climax. My juices erupted from my body as I squirted like a volcano awoken after many years.

"Finish her," was my command. I reached over and kissed him. My tongue danced in his mouth as he fucked her hard. He removed the condom and slid into her asshole.

Screams turned into moans and her voice echoed throughout the room and the sounds of his thighs slapping hers created rhythmic drum beats. I wanted him to fuck me next. I pulled her off of him and positioned myself so he was between my legs. I used her ass as a pillow. My weight trapped her as she struggled to get from beneath me. She wasn't going far.

Asher alternated between her ass and my pussy. I wanted to feel what she felt. As far as I was concerned we were living vicariously through each other. Was I worried about contracting something? No. My life was already filled with people emptying their bullshit inside of me so I couldn't be anymore corrupt than I was already. Asher entered me raw and I didn't mind. The nut was mine.

My body convulsed under his as I felt his emotion being inserted into my body. Sweat dripped from his stomach onto my thighs. I no longer cared about what my body looked like. He wanted me for me. Chemira began to squirm and move from beneath me. He removed his dick and stuck it inside of her for a few strokes to quiet her. She moaned and I felt her shiver. Her breath grew labored and I massaged my clit waiting for my turn to come again. It did.

Asher once again entered me and gripped my hips pulling them quickly to him. I wanted to make him want me more than he already did. Harder and harder our bodies thrusted and then he convulsed. I felt his dick pulsate on my walls and the hot spurts of his legacy coat my insides. I felt myself approaching climax at the same time and I bucked and shook under him. Chemira squirmed and climbed out from under my back with frustration. She stood near the bed and glared at the both of us.

"What the fuck was that about? Are y'all crazy or something?" She wiped the remnants of Asher's cum from between her legs. Her skin was blotchy due to the aggressive touches that we gave her as well as from anger.

Her eyes darted from his face to my body with regards to what she was going to do next. Chemira grabbed the sheet from the bed covering her naked body suddenly feeling vulnerable and naked in the emotional form to match her vulnerability in the physical.

"Don't stand there all high and fucking mighty like you didn't enjoy this. I know I did and you basically asked for it." I climbed off of the bed and sat with my legs crossed. Asher made his way past Chemira and she glared at him.

He stopped in his tracks. He realized what had just occurred. This could potentially be reported as a sexual assault. She was violated without permission. Her voice said no many times. Her body contradicted itself and we responded to that instead.

"Che, I'm sorry. It seemed as if you were a willing participant and you wanted to get down with us. You wanted to get down with me. We just simply obliged you."

"It doesn't fucking matter. Where are my clothes? I gotta get the fuck out of here." Chemira walked towards the door and stopped.

"You killed Kenton. He was here. I saw him walk in but he never left. Then I see you cleaning up and shit. I knew there was something wrong with you! You are crazy. Asher, how could you fuck with such a crazy bitch?"

Chemira grabbed her shorts and put them on one leg at a time. Her top she retrieved from the floor and she gathered up her bra and panties holding them in her hand. There was no time for putting them on. Her goal was to get out of there before she was also a victim. Her plans were foiled when I stood up.

"Yes, I killed him. You want to know why? Because he talked too fucking much. He always wanted to control what I did however I discovered my voice and the voice I found is about to tell you to sit the hell down before you're next."

I grabbed Asher's shirt off the nightstand and placed it over my head. My nipples stood erect and my body grew hot. Chemira walked back further into the bedroom and away from the door. She wanted to leave but my words frightened her. She stepped back and fell. Her face hit the floor and she wrinkled her nose. She smelled something. I looked at where her face was and it was in the exact spot that Kenton was killed. The jig was officially up.

Chemira stood up slowly. She wiped her hands on her thighs to try to remove the bleach smell. She looked at me and then down on the floor. The discoloration of the wood told the story that something was there. My heart started to beat rapidly.

"So that's where the blood came from? I thought it was wine or something. You really are a crazy bitch. The neighbors were right about you." Chemira stood on the same spot that Kenton had met his fate. There was something about my bedroom that made it hard for people to leave in one piece.

"Taryn what is she talking about? You killed Kenton?" Asher asked grabbing my wrists and making me look at him.

I didn't want to look him in the eyes. I was afraid he would see the monster that I had become. I hurt so I wanted others to hurt also.

"Yes the bitch is a murderer. No wonder people are seen coming in here but never seen leaving. This is like a fucking roach motel!" Chemira continued her tirade and Asher's eyes grew as wide as saucers. The room started spinning and getting darker.

"Chemira let's talk about this. There has to be a reasonable excuse for why Kenton and Edith have gone missing. Taryn would never do anything like that. Would you Taryn?" He turned to look at me.

I wanted to believe it myself but I knew the truth better than I knew the lies. I was an evil monster and I murdered people. My addiction for food had been replaced by my addiction for murder.

"Ain't nothing to talk about Asher. This bitch is crazy and if you are on her side you are just as crazy. She's not well and she's hurt everyone that's been in her way. You are slated to be next to die if you continue to stay around her. I love myself way too much to get caught up in the bullshit. I can't believe I never saw the signs. Now that I know, she's gonna kill me too." Chemira looked at me with fear in her eyes.

I smirked. I knew she would figure things out soon enough. She tried to bolt past me but I caught her in a headlock. She gasped and Asher ran to grab his pants. His back revealed the scratches that I had placed on him during our session. I wondered if he would still love me after he saw the monster that I had become.

"Just where the hell do you think you are going? You, my friend have just sealed your fate with your words. You think I can let you go home now after all you've seen and all that you know?" I whispered in her ear. My breath, hot and smelling like Asher's dick bounced off her neck causing me to smell it. It actually turned me on.

Asher walked over to me and tried to pry my hands from around her neck. I pulled away from him. She and I shifted to another corner of the room. I didn't want to let go. It was like I was holding her hostage yet I had no gun. Asher attempted to be the negotiator but he was only making things worse. There was no way that she would be leaving alive or without permanent damage.

"Please. Please Taryn. I am sorry. I promise that I won't tell anyone. Just let me go and y'all can have whatever freaky relationship you want. I don't want him. I don't need him. I just want to go home."

"Home? Everyone wants to go home when they are scared. When they walk into darkness that they know they shouldn't have, they all of a sudden seek the light!"

"Taryn please don't do this to her. Let her go," Asher pleaded with me but I ignored his requests. Either he was with me or against me and I was ready to take down whoever wasn't on my team.

Chemira's eyes bulged from the sockets as my hands continued to extract the life from her. She couldn't hold out anymore. Her last words whispered were, "Why?" and her eyes rolled in the back of her head nestled in the darkness that embraced her.

She was gone.

"Why did you do that? How are we going to hide this body?" Asher began to pace back and forth in horror. He hadn't ever seen a situation like this and didn't know how to handle it clearly. He was in the business of saving lives and here I was removing them bit by bit. This was my element and he was the visitor.

I bent down next to her and checked her pulse via her carotid artery. From what I could tell, she was gone. I then noticed her phone lay next to her. I wondered what was in it. Hopefully nothing incriminating or else we would be in big trouble.

"Do you know her password?" I asked Asher knowing he wouldn't have a clue but maybe he got close enough to see her input it. "I don't fucking care. I might be caught doing something. Help me or get out," I yelled at him. He began pacing and wiping the sweat off of his brow.

"There's no way to get into her phone. What are you going to do? Cut off her hand?"

Asher chuckled at the mere thought of me doing something so silly.

I stared blankly at him then went over to the side table to retrieve a pocket knife. I returned to my seat on the floor where Chemira lay and placed her hand straight out. Focusing on her thumb and forefingers I cut rapidly into the joints and removed the tips. I placed each of them onto the button of the phone.

Blood dripped down my hand and I wiped it on the white tee shirt I wore. My breasts contained red streaks that resembled paint marks. It wasn't so glamourous. I tried another fingertip and the phone opened. I dropped it to the floor and opened her photos immediately. My mouth dropped and tears welled up in my eyes. It was then that I knew my decision to end her life was one that could save mine......